SWATHWA VIPRASTHITHA
THE VOYAGE OF SOUL

JIJESH V SASEENDRAN

BLUEROSE PUBLISHERS
India | U.K.

Copyright © Jijesh V Saseendran 2025

All rights reserved by author. No part of this publication may be reproduced, stored in a retrieval system or transmitted in any form or by any means, electronic, mechanical, photocopying, recording or otherwise, without the prior permission of the author. Although every precaution has been taken to verify the accuracy of the information contained herein, the publisher assumes no responsibility for any errors or omissions. No liability is assumed for damages that may result from the use of information contained within.

BlueRose Publishers takes no responsibility for any damages, losses, or liabilities that may arise from the use or misuse of the information, products, or services provided in this publication.

For permissions, requests or inquiries regarding this publication, please contact:

BLUEROSE PUBLISHERS
www.BlueRoseONE.com
info@bluerosepublishers.com
+91 8882 898 898
+4407342408967

ISBN: 978-93-7018-169-4

Cover Design: Shubham Verma
Illustrated Design: Vijingovind, Shruthi
Typesetting: Sagar

First Edition: June 2025

Chapter 1

In room 116 of the city's multispecialty mental hospital, the noise and screams carried across the room and reached the staff room at the end of the corridor. Ramakrishnan and Sugunan rushed to the source of the sound. Room 116 was at the end of the corridor on the first floor. Ramakrishnan was trying to open the door by taking a set of keys from his bag. He had the keys to all 20 rooms on that floor, but amidst the worry, it was difficult to find the key for room 116. Pappan had fallen on the ground and screamed loudly, frothing and bleeding from his mouth. Pushing open the door, attender Ramakrishnan and nurse Sugunan rushed to Pappan. Ramakrishnan tried to hold Pappan by force and put him on the bed. He took Pappan's right hand behind his back, put one hand on his neck, and laid him on the bed. By that time, nurse Sugunan filled the syringe with medicine and injected it into Pappan's buttocks. His body trembled and groaned, his strength waned, and Pappan fell into a slumber.

****

Padmakumar was the only son of Shanti, the youngest of the four daughters of Madhavan Karanavar of Kunnath family. Padmakumar's grandmother, Janakiyamma, was the first to call him Pappan, which later became a nickname. Pappan had completed his B.Tech studies and was pursuing his Diploma in Visual Media.

Kunnath Tharavadu was a large Nalukettu compound. That ancestral home was centuries old. On the west side, behind the Nalukettu home, there were approximately ten acres of wetland. Beyond that was Bhagavathikunnu, the hill where Theyyam was observed.

Two days before,

Sitting amidst the fallen leaf litter inside the ¹kavu, Pappan said to himself while looking at a copper plate and holding it in his hand, "Gotta get it this time."

The sunset rays extended beyond Bhagwati hill. There were a lot of letters and symbols on the copper plate. Something vaguely written in small and capital letters was on it. It was a sketch—a sketch of the vault under the puja room at Nalukettu. Pappan rubbed lime on the copper plate and wiped it; the lines and letters on it became clear. What looked like "squares" were individual chambers in the vault. The primitive Malayalam script was also written in each square. The vault housed many centuries-old artifacts. Pappan's grandfather's grandfather had this vault built by carpenters and masons to store the antiquities.

---

¹**Kavu** is the traditional name given for sacred groves across the Malabar Coast in Kerala, South India.

There are even precious books that no one had seen before, one of which was *Swathvaviprasthitha*.

Pappan took his mobile phone, scanned the writings on the copper plate, and started searching on Google. He was able to understand the part written on the copper plate that said "North". Moreover, it was possible to determine in which chamber the object Pappan was looking for was located.

Raghunandan, the boy from the neighbouring house, called loudly while coming on his bicycle.

"I got it. I got it... Oh, he kept asking, what is this key? And where did you get it from?"

Leaning the bicycle under a tree, he walked towards Pappan and handed him the big key in his hand. Pappan looked at the key again and again, a big iron key about six inches in size.

"Where is the old one?"

Pappan asked Raghunandan without raising his head.

Raghunandan took out the paper wrapped around his waist and opened it. It contained a key with all its rusted teeth rotting away. Pappan double-checked his work with both keys.

Pappan said to Raghunandan as he got up from under the Elanji tree and walked out of Kavu with his keys tucked into his waist.

"You have to come home at half past ten tomorrow."

Raghunandan hesitated. "Then... there..?"

Pappan explained as he stepped over the Stone steps.

"Tomorrow is the day Surya[2]sankranthi. Everyone will go to pray at Bhagwati Hill and will return only in the afternoon."

That night passed. A crow pheasant called from the bushes beyond the kitchen. The sun was only getting hotter. A squirrel jumped out of the house from a tree branch. The location of the [3]puja room was beyond the atrium of the house.

The puja room was filled with copper pots, copper lamps, and scriptures. It was filled with the smell of sandalwood, camphor, and burning lamps with sesame oil. The floor of the puja room was made of wood. A lamp on a chain hangs near a large wooden storage box beside the right wall. Pappan placed the copper plate on the wooden box and pondered over it.

"Underneath this large wooden box is the passage to the vault."

Raghunandan and Pappan took hold of one side of the wooden box and moved it. Years of dust lay on the door. Pappan opened the cellar door with his left hand used the key. Vijakiri's noise and dust flew all over the place. Pappan instructed Raghunandan before starting to descend into the vault.

"Stay here, and I will try to come back in 10 minutes, max."

With the flash of his phone, Pappan descended the stairs into the cobwebbed cellar.

---

[2]solstice
[3]Prayer room

The cellar has been closed for a long time. There was a possibility of toxic gas.

He turned left after 8 steep steps, and there were 8 more steps. Reaching the bottom, he took out a lighter from his pocket, lit it, and looked around, checking for the presence of Sulphur gas. After taking a towel and tying it around his face, he searched around with the flashlight of his mobile phone. After 10 feet from the bottom of the stairs, two narrow corridors opened to the left and right. Pappan looked at the compass on his wristwatch and understood the direction of north. By taking the copper plate and aligning it with the north direction, an impression of the vault was made. After some thought, Pappan walked into the corridor on the right. There were small chambers on both sides. After four chambers, the corridor turned left. Breathing became very difficult as the air circulation decreased. Oxygen levels were very low. Pappan took a deep breath.

Pappan realised that he could stay there for a maximum of two more minutes. He had to get it within that time.

Walking forward again, Pappan stood in front of the second chamber in the corridor to the left. He took the copper plate and checked it with the flashlight of his mobile phone.

"Yes, this is it."

In front of him was a four-foot-high, double-panelled door. The door was locked. Pappan felt weary.

"How do I open it?"

His eyesight was beginning to decline, and his legs became weak. As he leaned against the wall and took a deep breath, the mobile phone and the copper plate fell to the ground. The sound of Pappan's deep breathing echoed through the cellar. When he inhaled for the third time, Pappan collapsed on the ground.

A spark of thought flashed through Pappan's mind when the flashlight of his mobile fell on the copper plate. He picked up the copper plate and checked it again. Three letters are written in the primitive Malayalam script on a copper plate, similar to the one column on which he stands.

Pappan knelt down and checked the lock. There were three rotatable rings, each engraved with numbers in primitive Malayalam script. Pappan rotated the rings and arranged them according to the numbers on the copper plate.

A screeching sound came from inside the lock. It opened. Vijakiri responded with a loud voice as the door was pushed open. Pappan was surprised by the sight inside the chamber. A light shone from many books inside the chamber, which might have been coated with a fluorescent substance. In the middle of the room, he found a distinctive box on top of a table. The following was written on the box below the carved image of the pig:

"Swathwa Viprasthitha"

****

Chapter 2

Dr. Alexander, a world-renowned psychologist, had made his theses available for study at many universities. The doctor visited the multi-specialty mental hospital where Pappan was admitted. Padmakumar's father's elder brother, Raghavan, and their daughter, Deepa, along with Raghunandan, sat on the sofa facing the doctor. The doctor looked at Raghavan over the spectacles on his nose and said, "I want to know a few things in detail. That is why you were called here. Padmakumar is now completely delusional. His conscious and subconscious minds are no longer active."

The doctor drew three circles on a piece of paper on the table and labeled them as conscious, semiconscious, and unconscious.

Turning the paper toward those in front of him, the doctor said, "The structure of our mind can be presented like this: It is in the conscious mind that we see, hear, and experience the world through the five senses. All dreams take place in the subconscious mind. Both of these minds are not currently active in Pappan's case. Due to the activities going on in his unconscious mind, Pappan screams at the top of his lungs. I think there must be a reason for this. There are reasons for everything in this world. There are reasons for even a leaf to move."

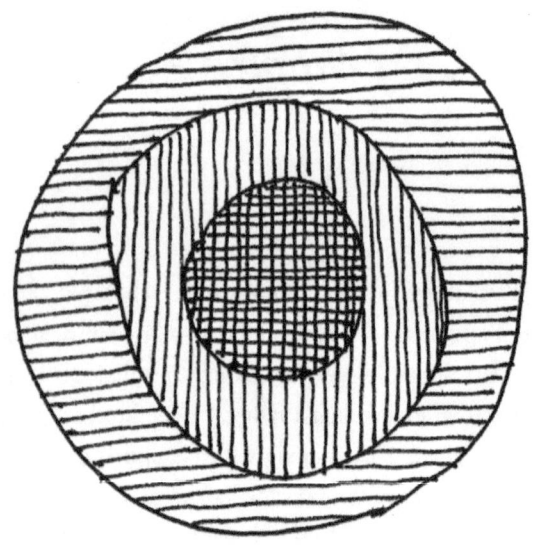

The doctor leaned back in his chair. Deepa looked at Raghunandan. Raghunandan looked at Deepa and Raghavan nervously.

"This is after reading a book," said Deepa.

"A book? Whichbook?" the doctor asked.

"*Swathwa Viprasthitha*"

The curiosity and surprise in the doctor's eyes flashed through the glasses onto the faces of the trio.

Raghavan sat up in his seat and said, "It is a book that was kept in the vault of our family home. That book, *Swathwa Viprasthitha*, is centuries old. It was written in AD 1600 by Brahmadevanandan, a yogi. Before I talk about the book, I need to talk about the author."

"It's interesting. Go on," the doctor said.

Raghavan continued, "His name was Pachan. Born centuries ago as the son of a tenant in our ancestral home. His father and mother were labourers in our fields. When the upper-caste children went to school, there was a desire for Pachan to study as well. For that, before dawn, Pachan and his friend Ambu would sit on the branch of the tree beside the school."

"Lessons in school were learned by sitting on the tree branch. Once, both were caught and made to kneel in the copra field near the house with their hands tied behind their backs. Pachan, exhausted by the heat of the sun, was startled by the loud cry of Ambu. As punishment for listening to the Vedas, molten lead was poured into Ambu's ear. The loud cry of Ambu shook the land. While preparing to pour lead into the other ear, Pachan jumped up and rushed toward Ambu. Pachan stomped on the hand of the man holding the lead pot. Molten lead splashed his face, and he fell backwards. By the time the others reached the scene, Pachan had already run. He jumped over the mud wall on the boundary and fled into the field, running over Bhagwati hill and further away from the land."

"Later, after a long time, he returned with the name Brahmadevanandan. During this period, he had traveled to many lands. He acquired much knowledge from many gurus and spent several years in penance in the Himalayas. From there, he learned Manovijnana, or present-day psychology, from a monk. He learned about the different levels of the mind, the voyage of the mind, and the control of the mind. It is also said that he visited the palace of Mughal Emperor Shah Jahan, where he debated with court scholars and received gifts from the emperor. He returned to his native land after many years of wandering. He built an ashram, and imparted knowledge to the low-caste children. It was a revolution—sometimes an unrecorded revolution in history. Brahmadevananda gained popularity among the people. Those who did not like it tried to attack him. But no one had the courage to face the fervor in his eyes."

"A conspiracy was formed against him. About 100 Mallans[4] were imported from Kaliyakavila in the south. They surrounded the ashram with the intent to kill Brahmadevananda. However, the spirit of the ashram frightened them. After a long wait, they set fire to the ashram. Brahmadevananda was also gone when the ashram burned down. He was burned without even becoming a part of history. But one thing remained: a box that was left inside the ashram did not catch fire. The casket in which the book *'Swathva Viprasthitha'* was contained. It later became an asset in our vault."

The doctor googled the word *'Swathva Viprasthitha'* on his laptop.
"I can't find the word *'Swathva Viprasthitha'* on Google."

"It is a rare book, Doctor," Raghavan said.

---

[4] fighters

Deepa added, "It has a strong magnetic field."

She was a lecturer in the Malayalam Department of Government College. She continued, "Through this, we can recognise the mental strength and ability of a yogi named Brahmadevanandan who lived in the seventeenth century. This book can steal our minds through hypnotism. If you chant the mantra *Swathva Viprasthitham Asthu*, written at the beginning of the book, 101 times, and start reading it, your mind will reach the land of Thali in the seventeenth century. The body here and the mind in the land of the scriptures will drift apart. The truth and the secret are that those who enter the book will never be able to return."

The doctor rubbed his chin with his left hand and thought. Deepa and Raghavan were deeply disturbed by the silence in the room. Even the movement of the second-hand on the clock could be clearly heard. As he leaned forward and scratched the back of his head with his right hand, the doctor said, "If he has such knowledge and consciousness and has written such a book, he must have found a solution to this problem." "What is the solution?" Deepa asked eagerly.

The doctor looked at the faces of the three: "I don't know, but the solution will be in that book, like a puzzle."

Raghavan's mobile rang before another silence began. As he answered the phone, Raghavan's brow furrowed, and his face looked very worried.

Raghavan found it difficult to speak because his breathing was so fast.

"My son, Rishi, is reading that book—the book *Swathva Viprasthitha.*"

Raghavan was the husband of Madhavan Karanavar's eldest daughter, Sarada, and their children were Deepa and Rishi. Rishi was 5 years younger than Deepa. He had completed his master's degree from the Amity Institute of Psychology in Uttar Pradesh and was currently pursuing his Ph.D.

The courtyard of Kunnath Tharavadu had dried up due to the sun. Raghavan, Deepa, and Raghunandan got out of the Innova, which had just reached. The doctor followed them. Rishi's friend James was standing at the door. Everyone made their way to the puja room.

Three lamps, lit with five wicks, spread light throughout the puja room. The smoke of sandalwood filled the room. Rishi was seen sitting on a wooden board in the light of a chandelier. In the attic, in front of him, the book *Swathva Viprasthitha* lay open. Rishi, dressed in light clothes with his eyes closed, had a special vitality on his face.

When Deepa attempted to prevent Rishi from reading, the doctor was involved and opposed. He whispered in Deepa's ears that it was more dangerous and let him continue.

Rishi's mind started the voyage.

'*Swathwa viprasthitha*'

'*Voyage of the Soul*'

****

Chapter 3

S wathwa viprasthitham Asthu

Swathwa viprasthitham Asthu

Swathwa viprasthitham Asthu

Swathwa viprasthitham Asthu

Swathwa viprasthitham Asthu

Swathwa viprasthitham Asthu

Swathwa viprasthitham Asthu

Swathwa viprasthitham Asthu

Swathwa viprasthitham Asthu

Swathwa viprasthitham Asthu

Swathwa viprasthitham Asthu

Swathwa viprasthitham Asthu

Swathwa viprasthitham Asthu

Swathwa viprasthitham Asthu

Swathwa viprasthitham Asthu

Swathwa viprasthitham Asthu

Swathwa viprasthitham Asthu

Swathwa viprasthitham Asthu

Swathwa viprasthitham Asthu

Swathwa viprasthitham Asthu

Swathwa viprasthitham Asthu

Swathwa viprasthitham Asthu

Swathwa viprasthitham Asthu

Swathwa viprasthitham Asthu

Swathwa viprasthitham Asthu

Swathwa viprasthitham Asthu

Swathwa viprasthitham Asthu

Swathwa viprasthitham Asthu

Swathwa viprasthitham Asthu

Swathwa viprasthitham Asthu

Swathwa viprasthitham Asthu

Swathwa viprasthitham Asthu

Swathwa viprasthitham Asthu

Swathwa viprasthitham Asthu

Swathwa viprasthitham Asthu

Swathwa viprasthitham Asthu

Swathwa viprasthitham Asthu

Swathwa viprasthitham Asthu

Swathwa viprasthitham Asthu

Swathwa viprasthitham Asthu

Swathwa viprasthitham Asthu

Swathwa viprasthitham Asthu

Swathwa viprasthitham Asthu

Swathwa viprasthitham Asthu

Swathwa viprasthitham Asthu

Swathwa viprasthitham Asthu

Swathwa viprasthitham Asthu

Swathwa viprasthitham Asthu

Swathwa viprasthitham Asthu

Swathwa viprasthitham Asthu

Swathwa viprasthitham Asthu

Swathwa viprasthitham Asthu

Swathwa viprasthitham Asthu

Swathwa viprasthitham Asthu

Swathwa viprasthitham Asthu

Swathwa viprasthitham Asthu

Swathwa viprasthitham Asthu

Swathwa viprasthitham Asthu

Swathwa viprasthitham Asthu

Swathwa viprasthitham Asthu

Swathwa viprasthitham Asthu

Swathwa viprasthitham Asthu

Swathwa viprasthitham Asthu

Swathwa viprasthitham Asthu

Swathwa viprasthitham Asthu

Swathwa viprasthitham Asthu

Swathwa viprasthitham Asthu

Swathwa viprasthitham Asthu

Swathwa viprasthitham Asthu

Swathwa viprasthitham Asthu

Swathwa viprasthitham Asthu

Swathwa viprasthitham Asthu

Swathwa viprasthitham Asthu

Swathwa viprasthitham Asthu

Swathwa viprasthitham Asthu

Swathwa viprasthitham Asthu

Swathwa viprasthitham Asthu

Swathwa viprasthitham Asthu

Swathwa viprasthitham Asthu

Swathwa viprasthitham Asthu

Swathwa viprasthitham Asthu

Swathwa viprasthitham Asthu

Swathwa viprasthitham Asthu

Swathwa viprasthitham Asthu

Swathwa viprasthitham Asthu

Swathwa viprasthitham Asthu

Swathwa viprasthitham Asthu

Swathwa viprasthitham Asthu

Swathwa viprasthitham Asthu

Swathwa viprasthitham Asthu

Swathwa viprasthitham Asthu

Swathwa viprasthitham Asthu

Swathwa viprasthitham Asthu

Swathwa viprasthitham Asthu

Swathwa viprasthitham Asthu

Swathwa viprasthitham Asthu

Swathwa viprasthitham Asthu

Swathwa viprasthitham Asthu

Swathwa viprasthitham Asthu

Swathwa viprasthitham Asthu

Swathwa viprasthitham Asthu

Swathwa viprasthitham Asthu

Swathwa viprasthitham Asthu

****

Chapter 4

Rishi was walking along the dark path. He felt as if he were trapped in a cave, withonly the cry of crickets and the darkness. He discovered a trace of light only after a long walk—a light from the cave entrance. Rishi walked toward it and slowly came out of the cave. Fog surrounded him. He waited for the sun to rise so the fog can dissolve. The birds chirped and flew off in search of prey. Rishi realised that he had reached the middle of a forest. He walked along a path covered with fallen leaves. Wrapping the thin shawl around his neck, he folded his arms and walked through the cold. Peacock feathers lay on the path. A vine tried to climb up a mango tree. Rishi felt as if many eyes were watching him from within the bushes. After walking a long distance, Rishi reached the edge of the forest.

The sun grew hotter. Rishi walked through a wide arecanut grove, where ripe arecanuts were falling. A small stream flowed through the middle of the garden. Beyond the arecanut garden was a vast paddy field. A kingfisher had arrived on a wheel near the field. A lamp hung from a stick stuck in the ground near the wheel. Children went down into the canal and caught fish with nets. By the time Rishi reached beyond the paddy field, the sun was overhead. A river was flowing beyond the paddy field; the sight itself gave a chill to the mind. A man was fishing in a small boat, andanother was selling vegetables and goods from a boat.

He felt refreshed when the cold wind blew. Rishi walked west along the banks of the river until he reached a market. A road passed between the river and the market. Two bullock carts were parked on one side of the road. Three-room shops lined the beginning of the market: aspice shop, a vegetable shop, and a shop selling iron metal goods. People came and went, buying things. The presence of women was minimal. A woman selling vegetables under a banyan tree, a woman selling fish, and a woman selling jasmine flowers a little further were the only women present.

There was a small hut beyond the banyan tree. Rishi approached it. An old woman, who had lost all her teeth, offered buttermilk to everyone. She scooped out some from an earthen pot with a wooden spoon and handed it to the Rishi. When Rishi drank the buttermilk, he felt chilled, even in every hair follicle. The cold breeze made him shiver.

A board was placed beyond where the lady was selling jasmine. It displayed a map of the land and some information about it. Rishi approached the board and examined it in detail. It was a map of a large area.

"How many lands can be seen like this?"

A little fear began to rise in Rishi's mind about how to find Pappan in these vast areas.

Rishi felt that the old man under the banyan tree was paying attention to him. He walked toward him while the old man was chewing paan.

"Kim avasyakam[5]?"

His language surprised Rishi. It was Sanskrit.

The old man asked again, "What do you need to know?"

Now Rishi felt relieved and asked, "I wanted to know about this country."

The old man spat the paan on the ground. He answered, "Let's say… Thali is the name of the country. A vast area stretching from Sahyadri to the Arabian Sea. This country can be classified according to topography as Kurinji, Mullai, Marutham, Neithal, and Palai. There are scholars for that in this country. Kurinchi means hilly area, Mullai means dense forest, Marutham is a combination of fields and land, Neithal is a coastal area, and Palai is the rainshadow land."

Rishi stood in front of him like a student.

"The kingdom of Thali consists of 18 such villages. Each village is about fifteen thousand acres."

He put two fingers over his lips and spat the paan onto the ground.

"Should I know where the capital of this country is?" Rishi asked.

---

[5]What do you want?

While looking to the left, the old man said, "Travel 200 miles south from here to reach the capital."

A servant came and stood in front of him after collecting the tax money.

"Was it collected from all stores?"

"Yes, we have it."

The old man wrapped his shawl around his neck, and walked with the help of his long umbrella. The servant followed.

Rishi asked loudly, "Can you tell me the way out from here?"

Old man chuckled and recited a hymn while walking:

"Anena Eva Ethath srushtam! Sa: eva thwam athra prapitha: Bhavantham athra sa: eva chairtha: cha! Bhavantham itha: preshayitha api sa: eva!"[6]

Rishi stood still there. The sun was beginning to lean toward the west. He went down the stairs to the river and took water in his hands to wash his face when he heard the sound of horses' hooves. Rishi turned and looked. An armed soldier on horseback rushed by. A horse-drawn cart followed, and the whole place was filled with dust. Rishi covered his face with his hands and tried to remember the beautiful scene that had just happened.

---

[6]"This place is created by the Creator.
It is the Creator who brought you here.
It is the Creator who has placed you here.
He is the one who will send you away from here."

A running horse-cart draped in red silk had small recessed windows on either side. The laughter of the girls inside the carriage echoed over the sound of the bells that accompanied the wheels. Two legs dangled from the cart, their beauty resembling moonlight. A fairly large black mole was visible under the right foot, behind the heel.

When Rishi opened his eyes, the chariot was far away. A soft feather fell on Rishi.

****

Chapter 5

Someone was singing loudly in a hut by the field. Like his song, the moonlight also flowed everywhere. A boy came with food to Rishi, who was lying on a rope bed under a banyan tree in the moonlight. He carried tapioca and kachil in an earthen pot, and crushed kantari for the cage. The boy returned to his hut, and there were five or ten huts side by side. Thatched huts made of mud; some of the houses had verandahs for children, and two adults carrying nets were walking towards the river. A few girls were sitting in a circle and slandering local news. An old woman sat in a sandy courtyard by the light of a lantern, plaiting a mat. A baby was sleeping at the end of the plaited mat.

After eating cassava and kachil, Rishi lay down on the stretcher. He fell asleep while watching the sky full of shooting stars. He woke up in the morning to the sound of the cock crowing, and as if he had made a decision, he started walking without stopping to ask anyone for permission. Heading west along the wide road ahead, the path before Rishi ended before a backwater lake as dawn began.

A small canoe was lying on the broad backwater pier ahead. Rishi got into the boat. He rowed the canoe across the backwaters. Rishi felt as if some invisible force was guiding him. No one could be seen on the banks.

On reaching the other side, he tied the canoe to the pole and walked again through the coconut grove. There was only the endless sea ahead. Rishi stood stunned in front of the immensity. His eyes, which had been looking at the sea for a long time, were full of tears, and when the waves went down from the mud in front of him, he felt that some letters were coming out clearly.

"Unless you know yourself, you end up here. In front of this immensity"

As Rishi looked, a powerful wave rushed towards him. Before he could take a step, the wave rushed over the letters on the floor and crashed down on Rishi.

****

Deepa was sitting on the couch in Kolaya[7], and the sadness of her mind was also visible on her face. The doctor, Rishi's friend James, and Raghunandan were in a closed room discussing something serious. Deepa ran from Kolaya to the puja room after hearing the sound of metal pot falling on the floor and the voice of the servant boy, Vijayan. Rishi had fallen unconscious and was lying in his mother's lap. By then, the doctor, Raghunandan, and James had rushed there. The doctor checked Rishi's pulse, opened his eyelids, and noted the movement of the pupils. BP was checked using a pressure monitor.

He said to James, "BP is too high. He should be taken to the hospital as soon as possible."

Deepa was stunned to see the last page of '*Swathva Viprasthitha*' opened on the board in front of the lamp.

"So maybe Rishi fainted after reading the last word of this book."

---

[7]Verandah

That truth silenced everyone present. Everyone could clearly hear their own heartbeat. The wick in the chandelier, which had been burning black, suddenly went out.

****

Rishi opened his eyes as sunlight hit his face. He was lying on the sand. Rishi got up and looked around at the calm sea. The place where those letters had been was now occupied by a conch shell, lying deep in the clear sand.

Rishi turned around without giving himself much time to think. He rowed the canoe and crossed the lake. He ran and walked back the way he had come: through the village, through the market, across the river, and through the fields.

When the sun set in the west, Rishi reached the end of the forest. He walked, looking at the signs he had noticed when he had walked before. Beyond the clumps of asparagus vines, and beyond the path where peacock feathers had fallen, he came to the cave from which he had descended. Even though light was dim, Rishi looked carefully. The front of the cave he had come down from was no longer visible. There was no evidence that such a cave ever existed.

Rishi felt darkness spreading in his eyes. As if his limbs were losing strength, he fell unconscious in the lap of the forest, where the dry leaves had fallen.

****

Chapter 6

Nani covered the steaming earthen pot with a wooden lid. The water from the porridge was scooped into an earthen cup with a spoon. She took two or three salt stones from another earthen pot hanging from the roof and walked outside to the verandah.

Nani was Koran Vaidyar's wife. Rishi was lying on a rope bed in their verandah. After placing the porridge water in the earthen cup on the half wall, Nani called Rishi.

He opened his eyelids and saw a thatched house with dung waxed on the walls and floor. One end of the verandah was covered with a straw curtain to block the bright sunlight. Rishi took the cup from Nani after sitting on the bed. With surprised eyes, Rishi looked at Nani and then at the surroundings of the house.

"Drink it; it's salty porridge water. All fatigue will go away."

Rishi felt refreshed after drinking the porridge water.

"Where am I...?" Rishi asked as he returned the cup.

"Manikyan, who went to collect honey in the forest, saw you. At first, he thought it was a snake bite. Since the man here is a vaidyar, Manikyan carried you on his shoulders and brought you here. There is nothing to fear. Vaidyar said that when you regain consciousness, just drink warm porridge water, and everything will be fine."

While Nani was talking, Koran Vaidyar came in. Handing over the cloth bag full of herbs to Nani, he took a pot from the half wall, washed his feet, and entered the verandah. Seeing Vaidyar, Rishi got up from the bed. Vaidyar spoke as he sat on a wooden chair in verandah. "Sit down; you must be tired."

Nani walked in with the bag. Vaidya spoke again while wiping the sweat from his body with a towel,"I'm not trying to ask but you can tell me, right?"

"My younger brother is somewhere in this land. He must be found. I am looking for him."

Vaidyar asked, leaning forward and placing a small shawl on his shoulder, "How old will your brother be? What does he look like?"

"He will be twenty-two in the coming month of Meda. He is six feet tall and has thick hair, like his mother. wooden-coloured skin and a large black mark below the left eye."

A flock of birds flew across the sky from the east.Nani heard Rishi asking about the sword as she stepped out into the yard and disentangled the peppers with her legs that had been left to dry in the sun. A gasp rose inside Nani. She suddenly walked inside, covering her mouth with her left hand to prevent the rye from coming out. Koran Vaidyar could sense the moisture in Nani's eyes. He silenced himself.

Koran Vaidyar told the story as they sat around the fire in the courtyard at night: his son's story.

"Kelan was a guard of the Tali royal palace and a skilled warrior. Sometimes, we need to talk about Thali Palace before discussing Kelan. Thali royal Palace has a story of its own. This palace was built in its present form during the reign of Dharmapala, a popular king. There was peace and tranquilly throughout the country. It was the golden age of the Thali kingdom. He was also extremely concerned about the health of public. The royal court was rich in scholars and artists. He had appointed a vaidyan[8] from village to village. My grandfather was the appointed physician in this village."

The wood caught fire again when the ash covering the coal was removed with a stick. The chirping sound from somewhere in the corner had not stopped yet. When Rishi looked, many fireflies flashed on the twigs of the mango tree.

Koran Vaidyar continued,

"The king was a very visionary person, and he prepared an administrative code for sustainable good governance ahead of his administrative reforms. Then the kings after him who ruled the country were also bound to follow this rule of law."

---

[8]physician

Rishi asked, "Is the royal rule still according to that administrative code?"

"If asked like that…" Koran Vaidyar paused and took a breath. "I will tell you."

"The Constitution book, invaluable one is placed on a pedestal in the middle of the palace court. Scholars in the palace can study or do research. There is a constantly burning lamp in front of the pedestal where the book is placed. If the book is misplaced, other than by turning the pages, the lamp will be extinguished by the south wind coming through the tiny window next to the terrace."

Rishi grew curious. "Hasn't that lamp been turned off yet?"

Vaidyar replied, "Extinguished. The lamp hasn't been lit since then."

A questioning look appeared in Rishi's eyes. After a moment of silence, the Vaidyar continued, "After Dharmapala, the kingdom was ruled by a king named Dheerapala."

"Why do the kings had the names so different?" Rishi asked, doubtful.

"They are the descendants of some northern dynasty… They conquered the land long ago. Today's kings are their descendants."

"Vijayapalan and Vikramapalan were the sons of King Dheerapala, with Vijayapalan being the elder brother and naturally the heir to the kingdom. At the same time, I also inherited my father's position as a Vaidyar. People liked

Vijayapalan Raja's rule, but since he had no children, he was troubled by the thought of who would be the heir. He always wanted good governance in the country. Bhimapalan wasthe son of his brother Vikramapalan. King Vijayapalan judged that Bhimapalan was not capable of leading the country due to his often-proven bad character."

"Bhimapalan and his father, Vikramapalan, started plotting against the King Vijayapalan. A group was formed to spread evil propaganda against the king. They tried to spread scandals and create conflict among the people. That year, due to the lack of rainfall, there was less cultivation, anda group of people began opposing the king.

One morning, the lamp in front of the Constitution Book in the administration hall was found to be extinguished by the wind that came through the small window in the balcony. On this occasion, Bhimapalan and a group of soldiers entered the palace and took Vijayapalanhostage, accusing him of having lost the Constitution book. Bhimapalan declared himself king, keeping the palace scholars silent. Vijayapalan was also ordered to be imprisoned."

"What people saw thereafter was the worst governance in the country. Violence increased. Starvation-related deaths grew larger. Women lost their security. King Bhimapalan was a notorious womanizer. All in all, anarchy prevailed."

There was a silence. A little bit later Rishi asked, "What is Kelan's Story?!"

Koran Vaidyar was at a loss for words. When the fire was put out, only the coals remained. They kept burning. Nani was sitting on the half wall of verandah, leaning on a pillar. The Vaidyar spoke after glancing at Nani.

"Her father, Raman, was a manful warrior in the mighty army of the Thali Rajya. He made an announcement on the 28th day of the celebration of, the little baby. Raman named him as Kelan. And he declared: 'Kelan will be made a warrior.' Kelan grew up and learned martial arts from Kalari. He became a member of the palace army. Kelan was assigned as a guard in the palace. It was at the same time that Kelan's marriage to Savitri, the daughter of his uncle, was arranged."

Koran Vaidyar stopped, looked inside, and said, "Isn't it a long time? Go to sleep."

Nani walked in from the moonlit verandah. Koran continued, "It was the day before Savitri's engagement to Kelan. On Tiruvathira day in the month of Dhanu, Savitri took a bath in the pool of Poomalakavu temple in the early morning. Since there was moonlight, Savitri walked alone to the temple. Before she could hear a movement near the wall of the temple and raise her voice to ask 'Who?', a black cloth fell over her head."

"Kelan's duty that day was to guard the Antapura door of King Bhimapalan in the palace. It was still half an hour before dawn. Just then, two soldiers came to the Anthapuram carrying a girl wrapped in a black cloth."

"'What is this?' One asked with a wry smile."

"'It's a piece of cake for king,' Other replied."

"Kelan stood across the path and said, 'No, this is not allowed here.'"

"The second soldier, who was also guarding the gate with Kelan, looked at Kelan with his eyes and gestured, 'It's better to allow it. .'"

"Kelan turned his face with angry eyes and reluctantly gave way. As Kelan turned around, a tender hand reached out from under the black blanket and grabbed Kelan's wrist.

"There was a tremor inside Kelan. He pulled away the black blanket with his other hand and saw Savitri, she was partially-conscious. One of the soldiers kicked Kelan when he tried to take his sword from scabbard at his waist. Kelan turned around from where he was falling and got up. Savitri was put on the ground, and the soldiers were prepared for a fight."

"Both warriors struggled to grapple with Kelan as the explosion inside his mind ignited a spark in his swordsmanship. A soldier's finger was injured by the blade of Kelan's sword, and his sword fell off. It was impossible for one person to face Kelan alone. The speed and the movement of Kelan's sword made the opponents shiver with fear."

"As soon as the sword was about to slash his opponent's neck,before the tip of the sword could reachhim, Kelan was slashed from behind. His body trembled. Kelan slowly turned around to look. The sword fell from the trembling hands of the soldier, who has been guarding with Kelan since long, to the ground. He folded his hands in front of Kelan and said, 'I'm sorry. I'm sorry.'"

"But Kelan collapsed.

When some water splashed on his face, Kelan opened his eyes and heard vague sounds, like those from a cave. His sight was disrupted by blurred vision and cloudiness. Kelan shook his head and looked around. There were five sword-wielding soldiers on either side of him who were tied to the stone pillar in King Bhimapalan's Antapuram. There was an excruciating pain in his back."

"'I forgive you. I do not punish your indiscretion. And a gift from King Bhimapalan for you this morning. May our intercourse with your bride be pleasing to your eyes,' said Bhimapalan as he let out a deranged laugh."

"Kelan gave a loud shout. He applied full force to break the chain attached to the pillar."

"After taking off the garments from Savitri's breast, Bhimapalan gently lay on top of her, pressing his body against hers. Kelan shouted loudly. Out of Antapuram, out of the palace, the whole country could have heard Kelan shouting. There was anger in Bhimapalan's eyes. While lying on the bed, Bhimapalan pressed his left hand on the ground and waved his right hand towards Kelan. From the speed of the hand, the dagger came lightning fast and stuck it on Kelan's neck!"

Koran Vaidyar stopped and bowed his head as he wept bitterly. Rishi's eyes were full of tears as well. After wiping his tears, Rishi just sat and looked at the sky.

****

Chapter 7

The sun was just coming up. Koran Vaidyar said, while walking down the stairs to the road, "I will also come to that junction."

Rishi, who retained his health, was set off from Koran's home. Nani looked at them while leaning against the pillar. Rishi was wearing Kelan's clothes: cotton pyjamas, a sleeveless dress with a red cloth belt, and a wallet around his waist. The wallet had been given to him by Koran Vaidyar.

There were horse hooves on the snow-soaked dirt road, and red flowers had fallen from the gulmohar tree. They walked and reached the junction where the three roads met. Koran Vaidyar pointed to the alley by the fig tree on the left.

He said, "I'm heading there. There's some nut to select. If you go down the road, you'll find a banyan tree near the pond. A nomad will be beneath the tree. His assignment is to travel the entire country. He might give you some tips, perhaps."

Swathwa Viprasthitha: THE VOYAGE OF SOUL

Rishi bowed to Koran Vaidyar. The Vaidyar raised his left hand, saying, "Good will come." Then, without looking at Rishi's face, the Vaidyar walked along the path by the fig tree.

Rishi moved along the muddy road and reached beneath the banyan tree. Next to it was a large pond with stone steps. Near the tree, there was a dull bundle of clothes and a bamboo stick. Rishi looked up after hearing the sound of whistling. Monkeys were jumping back and forth on the branches. When he looked at the steps of the pool, Rishi saw a man, wearing only kaupeenam[9], coming up the stairs from the pool. The old man, who appeared to be more than sixty years old, had a grey beard that reached his chest, and his matted hair was tied into a bun on his forehead. His toenails were long. He came to the banyan tree, took a dull cloth from his bundle, and put it on. He covered his body with another dull cloth. Without paying attention to Rishi, he muttered something under his breath, circled the banyan tree three times, and climbed onto a black stone to make a seat.

Rishi approached him.

"...I am...," Rishi began.

The old man put his finger to his lips and gestured for silence. A leaf fell between Rishi and the old man. Pointing south, in the direction where the tip of the leaf had fallen, old man said, "This is your way. What you are looking for is there."

Rishi raised his eyebrows excitedly and looked in the direction pointed out by the old man. A blooming bamboo forest. The

---

[9]Under wear

mud path ended at the forest; beyond that, the forest began. Unexpectedly, a bullock cart stopped in front of Rishi. Rishi got into the bullock cart full of copra along with the driver. After travelling through the forest, as dusk approached, they reached the land of Dashapuram.

The cartman said as he untied the oxen from the cart, "There is an inn nearby. We can stay there for the night."

By the time the bullocks were untied and tied to the nearby shed, the porters had come and unloaded the sacks of copra. Two or three people, dressed for a dance drama or something similar, passed in front of Rishi. The man, dressed as a girl, smiled at Rishi. A group of children followed them curiously. Rishi looked around and saw many houses beside the road. Behind them, he noticed a vast paddy field. A little distance to the left side, there was a rock hill with a small temple on top.

Rishi climbed the stairs and reached the top. There was no idol inside the shrine. A spring gushed from a small well. That point was the origin of the Thejaswini River. Rishi stood in front of the shrine. He went around to the left side of the shrine and reached the canal. Water flowed down from the shrine along a stone path. By the time the priest came out of the shrine with a camphor flame, the sun had already set on the western horizon. The wicks in the stone lamp in front of the temple spread light all around. A small copper pot was obstructing the flow of the spring from the sanctum, and a piece had fallen from the stone lamp. An apprehension flashed within Rishi.

"Has there been any trouble here?"

Rishi asked the priest, and after surveying the surroundings, the priest stared at Rishi's face again.

"Sorry, just a doubt of mine," said Rishi humbly.

The priest placed the plate in his hand on the steps of the shrine and walked with Rishi.

"A week ago, some miscreants came here. Those who covered their faces with black cloth had swords and daggers in their hands. They stopped their horses, climbed the stone steps, pointed their swords at the women who were there, and took money and jewels. One of them put a dagger to my neck, opened the locker in front of the shrine, and stole all the money from it."

Rishi could see an iron metal box with 'Vanchika' written on it lying near the steps on the south side of the sanctum.

"One of them has been caught. When all the others had gone on their horses, only one remained. Naduvazhi[10]'s guards caught him red-handed. He was tied to a bamboo stick near the stage in ground and beaten with a whip."

"Have you seen him?" Rishi asked.

"Yes, I also went to see him. He has a black mole under his left eye."

A lightning rushed through Rishi's guts.

---

[10]Local ruler

"He did not say a word about those who were with him, despite being asked by Naduvazhi. He gave the order to withhold meals from him until he provided details about the individuals in the group. Hasn't it been six days now without eating? He is sometimes seen as though dead."

Rishi felt fatigue weighing on him, but he regained his senses and ran. He went down the steps and into the street. Darkness surrounded him. The light from the lantern, which hung in front of the stage, crept over the darkness.

Under the neem tree, a man standing with a knot on his head, didn't noticed by Rishi Tightly gripping the horse's reins, the man fixed his gaze on Rishi.

Two people were standing on the stage, holding the curtain. Makeup was being prepared behind the screen. A few people had gathered in front of the stage. Rishi looked around places the light had touched. Children and elderly were among them. Rishi walked into the darkness behind the ground.

The man who stood under the neem tree mounted his horse and galloped away through the darkness in the lane.

Rishi was unable to hear anything else, as Chenda[11]'s voice from the playground was so loud.

A lot of fireflies were flashing here and there. Rishi stood, watching a firefly fly by him. In its course, the light suddenly disappeared, and there was something ahead. The firefly must

---

[11] Drum

have flown beyond that. Rishi rushed toward it. He hit the object in front of him.

A man was tied to a bamboo pole. The unconscious man had his head down. At the very first touch, Rishi realised it was Pappan, his younger brother. By the time he untied his hands, Pappan had fallen onto Rishi's shoulders. Rishi took Pappan's face in his hands. From somewhere, the small light of a flambeau fell on Pappan's face. As he watched, he felt that the light was growing, becoming a large glow. Suddenly, a bamboo stick hit Rishi's forehead. He lost his vision. He felt numbness in his head. And then, only emptiness.

****

Chapter 8

He could hear people talking, swords clashing, or something indistinct. Rishi tried to open his eyes, but he couldn't. He felt that he was lying on the ground with severe pain in his forehead, the pain spreads throughout his body. He suddenly opened his eyes when the water splashed over his head. Rishi looked around. He was inside a vast chamber. The ceiling was covered with straw. The ground was compacted and waxed with dung. The wallswere made of mud.A few people were there, training in martial arts. They were experts in sword play and churika[12]payatu. It seemed to be a Kalarithara. Rishi looked around again.

"Where is Pappan?"

Pappan was tied to the centre pillar of the Kalarithara.[13] By the time Rishi tried to sit up on his knees, Naduvazhi and his

---

[12]sabre
[13]The place where arms training

subordinates had entered the Kalarithara. Two men came,raised Rishi up, and made him stand in front of Naduvazhi.

"Who are the rest of your group? Where are they?" they asked.

Rishi threw his hand away from the soldiers and waved it toward Naduvazhi. He said, "You are mistaken. This is my younger brother. He is not a thief. I had been searching for him."

"There is no excuse for cheating and falsehood."Naduvazhi called in a firm voice."Kunga..."

A tall, healthy black man with a large scar on his left arm stepped forward. A scornful smile was on Naduvazhi's face as he said,"If you have the ability, you can save your brother. If not, both of your deaths will happen here."

Rishi opened his droopy eyelids and looked alternately at Pappan and Naduvazhi.

"This is the match for you."

Rishi looked down at the ground and saw two bows and arrows. The bowstring werenot tied.

"You can tie a string to this bow and shoot an arrow. You can cut the knot on your brother's hand with an arrow to set him free. You are competing with Kunkan. If Kunkan is the first to shoot the arrow, then the arrow is meant to penetrate the flesh of your younger brother."

As soon as Naduvazhi gestured with his hand, Rishi and Kunkan kneeled down in front of the bow. Rishi took the string and tied it to one end of the bow. His hand was shivering. By the time he bent the bow and tried to tie the string to the other side, it slipped out of his hands. Darkness spread all over his eyes while Rishi was trying to recover the bow that had fallen. Kunkan bent the bow, tied it at both ends, took an arrow and shot it towards Pappan. The arrow hit his right thigh. After a loud scream, Pappan lost consciousness again. Rishi closed his eyes tightly and turned away.

He begged on his knees in front of Naduvazhi, "Please have mercy; this is my younger brother. He is not the one who did the robbery."

Along with the laughter of those present, a disdainful smile spread across Naduvazhi's face.

He took the shawl in his hand over his left shoulder and made a sound by hitting it in the air. Rishi was shocked. Rishi and Kunkan lined up again with arrows and bows. Naduvazhi beckoned for the next match. Kunkan took the bow and started tying the rope. Rishi looked at Pappan blankly. Kunkan tied the string to the bow, took the arrow, and stood up, holding the bow in his left hand and drawing the arrow with his right hand. He aimed at Pappan's neck and pulled the arrow back as far as possible.

Before releasing his fingers from the stretched string, Rishi rose from the ground and stood against Kunkan, with the pointed end of the arrow in front of his neck. After blinking his eyes, he stared into Kunkan's eyes. Naduvazhi and those with him were completely stunned. Kunkan felt sleep in his eyes and lowered his hands slowly. Then Rishi turned to Naduvazhi.

"I am begging you again to be kind. You can punish us if we are found guilty. We are ready to accept whatever punishment you give us. Before that, I should be allowed to ask some questions of the officers who arrested Pappan."

One of the bodyguards stepped forward before Naduvazhi could give the command. Rishi asked, "Did you see the attackers going to the temple?"

"No, I was in front of the inn. I came running after hearing the noise and commotion from the temple."

"Then?" Rishi prompted.

"Before I could run, the assailants had run down the stairs and escaped on their horses."

"How many horses were there?"

"Six Horses."

"How many people were there?"

"Six People."

"Isn't there a man for every horse?"

"Yes."

"What was their attire?" Rishi continued asking.

"A black dress that clings to the body. The faces were covered with a black cloth, and there was a turban on their heads."

"Weapons"

"Yes, they all had swords in their hands, with a dagger at their waists"

Rishi moved in front of Naduvazhi and said, "These are the things that are clear from what has been asked so far. My younger brother was mistaken for an assailant and caught only because he was a stranger. The assailants who came there were dressed alike. All had weapons in their hands. Pappan's clothes are not like theirs. Pappan has no weapons. If Pappan had been a member of the gang, a horse would have remained."

Rishi respectfully continued in front of Naduvazhi, "I firmly believe that you are righteous. I have no doubt that no one who is innocent will suffer punishment in front of you." There was utter silence everywhere.

Few moments later, Naduvazhi finally said, "I have freed you both. But there is only suspicion that he is innocent, not proof. Therefore, I command you not to be seen in this land called Dashapuram again."

The silence continued.

Rishi slowly walked towards Pappan. His eyes were filled with tears.

****

Chapter 9

Pappan was lying on Rishi's lap as the horse-drawn cart moved along the deserted road. Pappan's head shifted with the movement of the carriage. His lips were cracked, and there was a scar around his eye. His eyelashes were clogged with dirt. It had been hours since they left Dashapuram Land. The horse-drawn carriage sped through the red-rock canyon, a desolate area with no houses or buildings—only scattered wormwood and venkana trees. The heat of the midday sun was oppressive. The cart driver stopped his horse-drawn cart near a ditch by the road. He untied the horses to let them drink. He went down to the ditch, scooped water into his palm, and drank as much as he could. The water was very cold.

He took a leather bag from the cart, filled it with water, and gave it to Rishi. Rishi wet a cloth with the water and applied a little to Pappan's lips. Exhausted by the sun, the wind seemed to lie down and rest somewhere. Even the edges of the grass were motionless.

"Which place are we going to?" Rishi asked the driver.

"To the place called 'Panchadasapuram'. It is to the east of where we just came from."

"How much further?"

"Maximum, two Nazhika.[14] We should be there in that time."

"My brother!" Rishi's words trembled.

The coachman spoke as he tied the horses to the cart, "Don't be afraid. We are going to the best treatment place in the country. There is a Vaidyar Math. They can provide any medicine. Sarngadharan is the chief physician. It is said he is a physician in the lineage of Dhanwantari. He is a Siddha who can even make anti-ageing elixir."

They continued their journey again through the sunlight. Sometime during the cartman's talk, Rishi fell asleep. They arrived in front of the Vaidyar Math at evening. A stream flowed on the right side of the road. Beyond the stream stood the Vaidyar Math, built like a Parnashala. A wooden bridge was constructed across the stream. Rishi carried Pappan and walked across the bridge.

When they arrived, Pappan were taken inside. After the Vaidyar descended from the Vaidyar Math, Rishi told him all that had occurred.

"Come on the morning of the fourth day; take your younger brother."

---

[14]Time denoting word

Rishi walked back across the wooden bridge and reached the road.

"I have to prepare a plan for the next three days; besides, I need to find a way out of here."

Rishi stayed at a nearby inn. The next morning, he bought a horse with a gold coin from his wallet and started his journey—a journey through paths he had seen before.

Bynoon, he reached a land where Rishi read from a sign placed on the street, 'Chaturdashapuram'. A plume of smoke was rising in a distance. Rishi felt that this place was very dirty compared to the streets he had seen before. Cow dung was scattered here and there, a rat lay dead in one place, and crows were scavenging on the scraps of food scattered along the road. Diseased stray dogs roamed around.

Rishi tied the horse to the stable next to the road and walked toward the market. All the markets he had seen before had special systems for draining sewage. But here, the stagnant sewage was full of insects and worms, and flies circled around the garbage. Rishi saw another sight there that was not seen elsewhere: a slave market, where people were sold at a price. The arms of five or six people were tied upward on a bamboo stick, attached to two pillars. People were kept on a platform. A woman was crying under the platform. Her son was also in that group.

"It is the beginning of destruction," a person who was standing near Rishi saw the scene in the market and said.

Rishi turned to face him as the man continued, "This practice was banned during the reign of King Dharmapala. He was the real king—a king who knew and loved the people. People enjoyed freedom then. Don't you see it now? People's freedom is hanging on a bamboo pole."

Rishi just shook his head as he listened. A tycoon and his servants arrived at the market. They began haggling over slaves.

Rishi posed the question, pointing to the smoke rising in the distance."Was there a fire?"

The man said with a sly smile, "As I said earlier, their freedom is burned, and the rest is smoldering.Each village has a village head, called Naduvazhi. The servants of the Naduvazhi of this village broke into the slave huts and looted them last night. They stole all the rice, coconuts, honey, and pepper they had stored. The hut of one of those who tried to oppose was set on fire. The people who were captured there are being hanged here as slaves."

Anger caused Rishi to feel the muscles in his face tense up as he asked,"Who tried to oppose them?"

"He is the one on the far left."

A person with a solid black body was tied to the left end of the bamboo pole. Blood was still flowing like yarn from his mouth. His lips were swollen and protruding. The scars from being beaten with a whip covered his body, but the bravery remained in his eyes. He looked around with a piercing gaze. As the tycoon bid him a price, Rishi walked towards them.

Unbeknownst to anyone, a man with a turban on his head stood by the side of the road, watching Rishi.

After throwing ten gold coins at the man selling the slaves, Rishi asked, pointing his index finger at the man on the far left, "I will pay ten gold coins for him."

One of the servants cut the knot of the slave from a bamboo stick, but the bond around his hands still remained. Rishi spoke in a firm voice, "The knot in his hands should be cut off."

The servant stood baffled.

Subran stated, "Do you want it? It will be difficult. He is more dangerous."

Rishi took the sickle for sale in front of the blacksmith's shop and cut off the knots binding Chantan's hands. He stood in front of him, hands still tied. Rishi whispered to him, "You are free now."

A sparkle of wonder appeared in Chantan's eyes. Rishi turned and walked away. Chantan followed him, bending forward slightly and crossing his hands. When Rishi stopped, hearing Chantan's footsteps, Chantan paused as well. Rishi turned around, raised his eyebrows, and asked, "What?"

Chantan shrugged and replied, "Nothing."

"You are free now!" Rishi said in a calm voice, one that only Chantan could hear.

Chantan's body bent forward a bit more as he said, "I will listen to whatever you, the Lord, command."

He had cried out for freedom when imprisoned. But when freed, he bowed his head at the door of imprisonment.

From the platform, Subran was again making the bargain, describing the qualities of the next slave.

Rishi's eyes were fixed on Subran. He placed the reaping sickle in Chantan's hands and said,"I will assign you a job. The knots on the hands of the rest of your group should be cut off."

Chantan looked at Rishi in surprise, while Rishi saw a glint in his eyes. Rishi whispered softly, so only Chantan could hear, "I bought you for ten gold coins."

A smile appeared on Chantan's lips, a grateful smile.

Chantan walked toward the platform with firm steps. Rishi called out loudly, "Your second job is to cut off the heads of those who are coming to oppose you."

The tycoon and his servants had already left the market. Subran and the man with him ran in two directions as Chantan rushed up to the platform with increased vigor. The gathered people cheered as Chantan removed the knots from each one's hands. An old man, who looked like a tribal head, Mooppan, approached Rishi. His voice was shaking and his grey beard couldn't hide his sorrows. His throat trembled as he said, "Lord, the tycoon will kill us, and they will burn our houses."

"Please look there." Rishi said, looking at the crowd dancing with joy at freedom."Their happiness is not because of good food, good clothes, or wealth, but because of freedom. Freedom is worth more than anything."

"Certainly, my lord, but our happiness will end now. Tycoon's people will kill us now."

Rishi said it with a smile, "I am not the Lord. I am a foreigner, not even your countryman. You have to do something. One of your group members should be called here, please."

Mooppan thought for a moment.

"Chantan..." Mooppan called loudly. As soon as Chantan heard the call, he stood in front of Rishi and Mooppan. Mooppan pointed to Chantan and said, "My son."

"Oh, he's smart," Rishi said and patted Chantan on the back. Chantan, who had been bending forward, suddenly straightened up. Holding Chantan's chin and lifting him up, Rishi said, "You should stand straight like this; your head should not bow in front of someone else. Look at those people. Didn't you see the happiness spreading on the faces of many who have never smiled before? Don't quench their smiles."

"The tycoon's attendants will undoubtedly arrive to silence your grins. It's not only for harvesting that I was holding in your hand earlier—the scythe. Perfect for pulling weeds as well. Hear what I have to say, then. There are over three hundred of you assembled here, excluding the elderly and the young."

"Call everyone who is at home and who has gone to work. The servants of the tycoon may be seen by only ten or fifteen people. If they attack you, hold back. Strike back with the weapon in your hand. This is your soil—the soil you were born into. You are the one who work on this soil. Every crop that blooms here belongs to you and your children."

Chantan looked at Rishi in surprise.

Rishi smiled and whispered, "Time is very precious now."

"Yes, I will," said he ran to the crowd.

A man, observing Rishi, suddenly galloped his horse towards the east.

Chantan called the children and sent them to each house. He handed the scythes to each one and shouted something loudly in their vernacular. Special care was taken to send the elderly to the hut.Some of them sharpened the ends of the bamboo sticks at Chantan's direction.They were ready. They took up positions in the market's courtyard, armed andready to fight for freedom.

****

Chapter 10

Rishi looked at the street as if expecting something. Birds suddenly chirped and flew away from the branches. A cloud of dust arose from the end of the line. Chantan turned the cold that formed inside him into fire. He gripped the bamboo stick tightly in his left hand. A scythe was tied at the end of the bamboo stalk. Like a storm, twenty or so of them—the soldiers of Naduvazhi—rushed in.

They held swords and whips in their hands. The sound of horses' hooves echoed like a war trumpet over the people. Everyone looked at Chantan and waited for his suggestion. Suddenly, Chantan ran toward the army, shouting in tumult, and his people followed him. About three hundred native residents surrounded the army of fifteen or fewer men. Although many were cut by swords and struck hard by the blows of whip, they fought. A brave fight for their freedom.

It was impossible for the soldiers of Naduvazhi to fight against more than 300 armed residents. Many soldiers were mortally wounded by the sharp edge of the scythe and bamboo spear. They had no choice but to retreat. Shouting, the locals pursued them for a while. Chantan could not believe that they would win so soon. He was picked up by someone, and there was an uproar of joy. The happiness of victory. The happiness of freedom.

Rishi and the tribal chief were standing in the middle of the market, witnessing the brave war.

Chantan stood in front of Rishi and folded his hands. "Now I am standing before you, not as a slave, but out of respect."

Rishi moved a little further and stood. He asked, "Have you ever heard of birds caught in a hunter's net?"

Chantan shook his head.

"There was a group of parrots in a forest. The parrots were flying around, picking rice from the field and picking figs and black plums. There was no limit to the sky for them to fly. They could eat food from anywhere. They could fly wherever they wanted; they could nest wherever they wished, while a hunter sowed rice and spread a net over it to catch them. The parrots that saw the rice flew there and got stuck in the net. The parrots couldn't do anything but hang around and condemn themselves. They did not even think they were going to become the prey of the hunter. A kind of callousness. A pigeon noticed the parrots entangled in the net as it flew by. The pigeon convinced the parrots of their dangerous situation. It also told them a way to escape. The parrots exchanged messages with one another. They chose to take off together. From a distance, the sound of the hunter's horse's hooves could be heard. All the parrots were ready. Together, they flapped their wings simultaneously and rose into the air. Thus, they were freed from the net."

Chantan stepped forward and said, "Lord, you are the pigeon that saved us."

Rishi laughed.

A girl came with a wooden tray. On it were wild honey in a bamboo tumbler and some figs on a leaf. She held out the tray toward Rishi. Rishi smiled and took a fig, tasting it. The tribal head poured some honey into the tumbler and handed it to Rishi.

The honey's heaviness began to catch at his eyelids. He started to feel dizzy. Yet again, Rishi addressed them, a smirk twitching on his lips.

"All the wild honey here is now yours. All the rice grains in this field are now yours. The water in that river is yours..."

One of Chantan's friends intervened and said to Rishi, "But they will come soon."

"Who?"

"People of Naduvazhi!"

"If they are coming to attack, resist," Rishi said.

"They will come with a lot of people."

Rishi smiled and looked around. There is a question and fear reflecting on everyone's face.

Rishi asked, "What's your name?"

A nearby man replied, "Raman"

Rishi put his hand on Raman's shoulder and asked with a smile, "Do you like jackfruit? The honey-filled jackfruit?"

"Yeah."Raman nodded.

"How much jackfruit can you eat in one sitting? A whole one?"

"If it's honey-filled, I'll eat even more."

Those standing around laughed.

"Raman, can you eat two whole jackfruits?"

"It's not... it's not all that much."

"Shall I place five full jackfruits before you? As you said, honey-filled jackfruit. What do you say? Raman, can you eat them?"

"Oh no."Raman felt himself shrinking.

Rishi asked the others, "I'm posing the same query to you. Could you...?"

No one responded.

Rishi said again, "I am going to announce a gift. If you eat all five jackfruits within half Nazhika, you will get one hundred bags of rice, one hundred bags of pepper, and one hundred bags of gold coins."

Rama sat up straight. Sparkle in the eyes. Excitement on the face.

Rishi asked Raman, "Are you ready...?"

"Yes."

The same excitement was on the faces of those around.

Rishi clapped and addressed everyone, "How quickly the phrase 'impossible' swiftly transformed into 'possible.' Raman's mind was distracted by gold coins, pepper, and a lot of rice. Our minds are prepared to take on any challenge and accomplish anything if a significant treasure is within our reach. Here, freedom is the treasure that is going to fall into your hands. Freedom to harvest what you sow. Liberty to make use of these forest reserves. Freedom to avoid bending down before others. Now tell me, don't you want to own this treasure?"

All of them, together with Raman, said,"Yes, yes."

"For that, you have to build a fort here—a kind of fort that no one else can invade."

Chantan's facial muscles tensed. Chantan thought to himself, "Even if hundreds of people come, we will fight. The attackers will be chased away."

That thought kept burning in many minds. Rishi realised that the light of that thought was reflected on every face.

As the western sky began to turn crimson, Rishi bade farewell to the tribal head and Chantan and rode his horse southward.

****

Chapter 11

The waves of moonlight spread like smoke all over the place. Silver clouds drifted between the moon and the stars. Along with the drops of the moon, snowdrops fell on the rock where Rishi was lying. Big bubbles flew through the air as if someone had blown them. The bubbles that flew from the sky burst before reaching the ground, and colored pearls fell from them. The rock was covered with multicolored pearls. In the light of the lightning, the shells of the pearls burst, and tendrils emerged. Slowly, they began to grow and get bigger. New leaves sprouted. New shoots grew from the stem. The buds at the end of the stem blossomed into flowers. The flower with many petals.

Rishi got up and looked around; the place was full of plants with many-colored flowers. Two baby rabbits rushed between Rishi's feet. A cloud broke apart in the sky and began to descend gently. Small clouds fell under Rishi's feet. Underneath the colorful flowering plants, the cloud was as soft as a cotton ball. A lot of fireflies flew there with the gentle breeze from the south.

As they landed on the petals of each flower, they turned into sparkles of different colors.

Along the path where the rabbits had run, Rishi also walked. Rishi came to a large pond with stone steps and a branch of a kadamba tree leaning over the pond. The baby rabbits that rushed under the kadamba tree suddenly hid somewhere. Rishi also reached beneath the branch of the kadamba tree. Some pieces of moonlight fell everywhere through the tree branches. Waterlily flowers bloomed all over the pond.

Two or three girls were sitting on the stone steps, laughing and chatting. A girl who looked like a goddess was swimming in the pool, along with the moonlight. Rishi felt that she must be an angel.He watched as she walked up the stone steps after her bath. Rishi stared at her wet body. A black mole could be seen on the backside of her ankle. She wore a pair of silver anklets. Suddenly, Rishi felt as if the soil beneath his feet was collapsing. Rishi fell into the middle of the water lilies in the pool before he could grab the branch of the kadamba tree.

****

Chapter 12

When a drop of dew fell from the leaf tip to Rishi's eyes, he jumped up in shock and looked nervously at his hands and body. The sun was just rising, but the crescent moon still hung on the western horizon, not yet set. Yesterday, Rishi had fallen asleep while sitting under the wormwood tree. He looked around. The grasses bent forward under the weight of the snowdrops. The sparrows perched on the branch of the wormwood tree and began chirping. A cowherd boy walked through the path beside the tree, leading five or six cows.

Suddenly Rishi noticed something.

"The horse is missing."

Last night, the horse had been bound to the root of the wormwood tree.

It was a vast area, with only sporadic wormwood and venkana trees, and stretches of laterite rock visible. Nothing else. But the horse was nowhere to be seen. Rishi carefully searched the entire area. Then, he noticed horse dung spread out in the distance. Beyond that, the Emban grass was trampled by the horse's hooves.

After glancing at the signs, Rishi turned and movedalong the side of a row of Venkana trees and Munda plants. The flat area sloped steeply at the end. Rishi made his way down the rocks.The plants along the pathwere blooming with pale blue flowers. A stream flowed down from the cliff along the edge of the vine-covered area.

Rishi walked further down. A pond appeared beyond a Kanikonna[15] tree full of flowers.It was a forest, full of flowering shrubs, vines, and large trees.By the pond, Rishi found his horse, close to a kadamba plant. In his dream, he had seen the same pond and the same steps made of laterite. Rishi gasped.

As the sun had risen, the amber flowers had withered. Rishi looked around but didn't see anyone in the pond or on the steps. He descended the steps to the pondand washed his face. It was very quiet there.As he was returning up the steps, he saw a single anklet lying loosely on one of the rock steps. He recognized the silver anklet; it had caught his eye before. In his dream. He picked it up.

Rishi turned around as he heard a horse neighing and saw a man fleeing from there. The man wore a mask. Rishi placed that anklet at his waist and sprinted to his horse. The moment the strange mansaw Rishi coming, he fled on his horse. Rishi mounted his horse and followed him.

---

[15]Cassia fistula

"It has come to my attention that he has been following me several times. Hisface is always covered. Who is he? What is his intention? Something remains a mystery."

****

Brushing away the flowers that had fallen into her hair with her left hand, Chitrangana looked out from the vine hut through the leaves.

"He has gone."

Chitrangana was the daughter of Gaurirani, who was the daughter of King Dheerapala of the Thali kingdom. Chitrangana had traveled far from the palace to the well-known Amber Pond early this morning with her companions Mayadevi and Vanidevi.

She went out of the vine hut with her companions.

"You still haven't said what the matter is," Maya said nervously. "Why did you come here early in the morning with us?"

"Oh sure, let's go to the root of that tree."

They sat on a root under a large tree. Chitrangana looked around, ensuring no one else was there.

"I had a dream this morning," she said.

"What dream?"Vani asked curiously, though her face was sleepy.

"Don't be in a hurry! I'll tell you..."

"Ok, no hurry."

"A night with snow and a moon. White amber blossoms in the pond. A handsome man was standing beneath the kadamba tree by the pond. The moonlight fell on his body through the leaves. Then, I was swimming in the amber blossoms."

"Didn't that Gandharva see you?" Maya inquired as she picked flower petals from Chitrangana's hair.

"Yes. Our gazes met. He was staring at me as I walked up the stairs. I was embarrassed. I hurried up the stairs."

"And then..."Vani seemed anxious.

"Then nothing. The sound of birds chirping kept me awake. That was the end of the dream."

Maya asked teasingly, "Is that Gandharva here now?"

Chitrangana's cheeks reddened; she blushed as she said, "Hmm… The Gandharva in my dream has the same face."

Maya seemed to recall something, "Isn't that Gandharva's hand holding your silver anklet now...?"

Chitrangana shook her head and smiled."That anklet will bring him to me."

A gentle breeze blew through the area as Chitrangana used her fingernails to scribble something on the root she was sitting on. She was daydreaming with her eyes open.

****

Chapter 13

If you looked from far above, it could be seen that the length of a line of dust was increasing over the land of laterite rock. Rishi was chasing someone else on his horse. The sound of horses' hooves and the splashing gravel spread everywhere. They rushed along the path through the rocky land, one after another. Rishi was unable to see the stranger ahead of him clearly because of the rising dust cloud.

The stranger kept going, descending the steep slope from the rock hill, rushing along the banks of the Tejaswini River, and speeding through the forest path strewn with fallen leaves. Rishi followed him in the same way. The man pursed his lips and whistled distinctively as he raced through the darkest forest path. He was trying to keep a constant distance from Rishi.

Unbeknownst to Rishi, another armed man had begun to chase him after hearing the whistle. A little later, two other persons also began following him. When the strange man reached a desolate meadow after passing through the forest, he skillfully stopped his horse to face Rishi. Rishi also stopped his horse by pulling tightly on the reins. Rishi then noticed that about five armed men had been following him.

They surrounded Rishi. There was no other choice but to obey their instructions. Rishi had to walk with them from the meadow to the steep, rocky area. There was a large cave on the slope of the hill. Leaving the horses outside, they entered the cave. A collection of weapons like swords, spears, hammers, and urumi in tiny rooms inside the cave could be seen. A ray of light entered the cave through the gap in the rock, and behind that stood a succession of men in the same uniform.Everyone was looking at Rishi. Rishi also looked at everyone. No one said anything.

"I don't know why you brought me here. I'm not the person you want. Actually, I am not really from this land. I'll tell you one more thing if you're not shocked. I'm from beyond time."

Their eyes were filled with wonder. They muttered something to each other. Someone took Rishi's hand and made him sit on a chair-like stone.

"Welcome to the country of Thali. We are the Serchas. We have a Guru.[16] That great sage's name was Brahmadevananda Yogi. Thali is in great danger today. According to the Guru, someone would cross time and space to protect the Thali territory."

Rishi was surprised to hear the name Brahmadevananda from them. Many things they said confused him.

---

[16]teacher

"Did you expect me?" he asked.

"We have no other choice. Our Guru had predicted that there would be many changes on your arrival. The changes in Chaturdasha Puram are proof of that."

Rishi chuckled to himself. He said, "I repeat, I am not the person you are looking for."

They whispered to each other.

"I would like to know," he continued, "What is Sercha? Who are you really? Why are you gathered here secretly?"

One man sat on another stone in front of Rishi. It was Ambadi, the head of the Serchas. He explained, "Serchas are a law enforcement group formed during the reign of King Dharmapala. Serchas have nothing to do with the army. The army fights with other countries and protects the borders. Serchas only interfere in internal affairs. The Serchas are responsible for preventing attacks and atrocities within the country, as well as fraud, extortion, and murder. After Bhimapalan came to power, the Serchas were dismissed. Then after anarchy prevailed in the country."

Rishi's thoughts drifted in a different direction, "If the king dismissed the group called Serchas, wouldn't such a gathering be anti-royal?"

Ambadi went on, "Restoring decent governance to the nation is our goal. Peace and tranquility must always prevail among the people, and the Serchas will continue to fight for it. It was during my grandfather's time that a law enforcement group called Serchas was formed. After my grandfather, my father continued the same profession. The Serchas were divided into groups and assigned to each village. My father was the head of the Sercha team in the capital city. During my father's tenure, there was no weed, robbery, or fighting in that land. I grew up watching this and wanted to be a good Sercha."

"What is the reason for the King to dismiss the Serchas?"Rishi inquired.

"King Bhimapalan came to power through cheating. Therefore, he left his subordinates to their own freedom. The Serchas were shackled for their anti-people policies, so such a group itself was banned. With that, the prosperity of the country was erased."

Ambadi stopped for a while. Then Rishi asked,"I've heard everything you said. What can a common man like me do about it? Choosing me as your savior is wrong."

Ambadi replied,"There are signs. Signs are always correct."

A man approached and whispered something in Ambadi's ear.

Ambadi said while getting up from his seat, "If it's okay with you, let's go meet the Guru. The horses are ready. One can see him only by entering the thick forest."

Outside the cave, the rays of the sun began to warm up.

Apart from Rishi and Ambadi, two others mounted horses and galloped towards the east. After some time, they reached the boundary of the forest. Stopping their horses near a well, Rishi and Ambadi entered the forest. Two others guarded the horses. Grasping the sword hilt that hung from his belt, Ambadi moved forward along the forest path. Pushing away the creepers with his hands, Rishi followed him. Their bodies felt the chill of the forest as they stepped into it.

Along the way, among the roots of a forest tree, a python's skin lay. Monkeys dangled from vines while squirrels leaped from tree branches. As they entered deeper into the forest, they could see the enormous trees. An owl stared at them from inside a tree trunk. After crossing a root-covered mound and clinging to rough black rocks, they walked through dense clumps of bamboo and came to a cave. Hearing the footsteps, the two baby rabbits inside the cave ran back to their burrows.

On the path where the baby rabbits went, a saint-like man sat under a banyan tree. A wondrous radiance shone on his face. Brahmadevananda opened his eyes and walked toward them. Rishi bowed his head and greeted him. Brahmadevananda asked with a proud smile, placing his hand on Rishi's shoulder.

"Rishi...isn't it?"

Rishi simply nodded.

"I introduce myself. I am the creator, who does not get salvation because the creation is not perfected yet."

Brahmadevananda invited them. They climbed the cliff through the rocks beside the cave. The mist wrapped around them like a thin blanket. The entire forest was covered in a misty shroud.

Brahmadevananda said, looking around, "A beautiful country was my idea, a country full of peace and tranquility. A land where all people are equal but..."

Brahmadevananda continued, folding his icy hands together, clenching his fists to his mouth, and blowing softly through them,

Pointing his finger at Rishi, Brahmadevananda said, "But there was an error somewhere in my work. Many letters were not picked up as I wanted. However, it is necessary to determine what can be restored. Occasionally, you will be assigned to undertake that task."

Rishi moved a little further and asked, "What do you expect?" Brahmadevananda kept rubbing his palms.

"If it becomes the kingdom of my imagination, someone must retrieve the lost book *Bharana Niyamavali*, the book of constitution, which was lost in the royal palace. It is certainly not completely destroyed; it may be hidden. The book must be found and returned not to the palace—but to the people. It is precisely defined on the last page of the *Bharana Niyamavali* how to elect another ruler when the monarchy in the land is broken. The government is governed by one of the people elected. He is not an authority but a servant of the people, and the book *Bharana Niyamavali* had not reached the people for so long so that they would not know its contents. Now, it was smuggled."

With a firm voice, Rishi said, "Are you implying that this is my mission? It isn't feasible. I'm not capable of doing this."

Yogi Brahmadevananda grinned. "Karma will have to determine whether it is possible or not. Do the Karma first. Subsequently, we can determine whether this is feasible. Everyone who comes here has a mission to complete. Your mission is to save the country from chaos and find the book *Bharana Niyamavali* for it."

Rishi remained silent, thinking many things in his mind.

"I will take on the mission, but you should be kind enough to tell me a way out of here."

Brahmadevananda laughed. Although the laughter dissipated in the fog, he did not stop. He kept laughing again.

"The only way out of here is the vessel of death."

Brahmadevananda laughed, as walked into the mist, and disappeared. His laughter echoed and melted away with fog.

****

Chapter 14

Rishi was thinking of something else even as Pappan was being taken away from the Vaidyar Math in a horse cart. Pappan sat silently.

Rishi thought about Brahmadevananda.

'How did he come to the land? What happened to him when the Mallans from Kaliyakkavila set fire on the ashram?'

At night, without even the light of a torch, about a hundred fighters surrounded Brahmadevananda's ashram. Lamps were hung at all four corners of the ashram. The light from the hanging lamp gave the ashram a special vibe. No one dared to trespass inside the ashram or oppose Brahmadevananda. One among the group lit the flambeau and threw it on the roof of the ashram.

When the fire broke out, Brahmadevananda saw through the window that the fighters were huddled around the ashram. Many people held sticks and daggers. By then, part of the roof had collapsed from the fire. Brahmadevananda took out a book, kept in the puja room: *'Swathvaviprasthitha.'* Each page of the book was smeared with a special ointment to prevent fire.

As the heat increased, the fire assumed a monstrous form capable of devouring anything. After a few more seconds, the rest of the roof collapsed. Before that, Brahmadevananda sat on a wooden board and began reading *Swathvaviprasthitha*. The fire then spread throughout the area. The heat and light from the fire engulfed everything. After reciting *Swathva Viprasthitham Asthu* a hundred and one times, the roof fell like a fireball. Within seconds, everything burned. Except for the book 'Swathvaviprasthitha'.

When Rishi opened his eyes in shock, the horse cart reached Serchas's secret sanctuary. Ambadi waited for them both. Ambadi greeted Pappan with folded hands.

"Welcome to the secret sanctuary of the Serchas."

However, obscurity clung to Pappan.

"We have a lot to talk about. Come..."Rishi said, patting Pappan's shoulder.

The cloud that had flowed with the southern wind rested and then flew north. Sitting on the rock atop the hill as the red sun slowly set, Rishi explained many things to Pappan: about the land Thali, about getting here, about the Serchas, and so on. A white egret flew from the field and perched on a nearby tree branch. Darkness began to spread slowly.

Pappen watched the egret, its white color fading and merging with the dark. As night deepened, the voice of the Great Pied Hornbill echoed in the wind. Inside the cave, the campfire began to die out. Still, they remained deep in a serious discussion. Rishi, Pappan, Ambadi, and other Serchas sat around the bonfire.

"So far, you have talked about the current regime, the king, the anarchy, and the state of the Serchas... that's all. Will the current problems be solved by just discussing the same issues back and forth? If you understand where the problems started, the solution will be clear. According to the Brahmadevananda yogi, the Bharana Niyamavali must be found. That was lost from the palace. Bring it back, and all the problems will be solved..."

Everyone listened attentively to what Rishi was saying,

"Really, what really happened? You may know many things that are clear. This issue needs to be addressed. That is the need here."

Ambadi, sitting next to Rishi, pointed to one of them and said, "Kunthan; Kunthan's elder brother was one of the palace servants. Thus, Kunthan knows some truth.

Kunthan rose from his seat.

"My elder brother's name was Kannappan. During King Vijayapala's reign, separate bodyguards were assigned to each member of the royal family in the palace. Kannappan was assigned as Vikramapalan's bodyguard. The same position was maintained during Bhimapalan's time. I met Kannappan the day before King Bhimapalan came into power. He told me something unfortunate would happen. Kannappan and another bodyguard were instructed to secretly take two men into the forest and kill them there. One of them was the carpenter. He added that he wanted to save our country. I never saw my brother again after he said goodbye that day."

The bonfire reflected in the tears that filled his eyes. The sound of the bird stopped. There was deep silence. In the dark, only the sound of crickets be heard.

****

Chapter 15

Pappan asked Rishi from neck-deep water in the river before the morning sun rose, "What are you thinking?"

"Right where we left off last night..."

The river water was very cold. A cuckoo sat in a nearby tree and sang. Rishi then slowly moved down into the river.

"What is your assumption? What should we do now?"

"This is a big question," Rishi said.

"I will tell you what happened, with a possibility or speculation."

"Vikramapalan and his son Bhimapalan were two people who did not like Vijayapala's reign becoming popular. They tried to stage a coup. If Vijayapalaraja were removed in any way, another system of governance might follow, as prescribed in *Bharana Niyamavali;* the ruler would be elected by the people. Thus, there would be no possibility of Bhimapalan being administered. Knowing this, Vikramapalan and Bhimapalan planned to destroy the book."

"And then?" Pappan asked eagerly.

"The palace was highly secured. Only highly skilled people could steal the book. Who could they be?"

"Surely, they might have been thieves."

"There are two possibilities."

"What are these two possibilities?

"First, they were expert thieves. But it was unsafe to entrust this work to such gangs. In the future, there could be blackmail because of this. Second, they might not have been thieves. Any mistakes were blamed on them, and they were called thieves."

"What is the underlying theory?"

"Simple. It is easy to intimidate these people. If executing them after need, there is no need to fear anything else."

"So, who were they?"

"Kannappan might have tried to save the book Bharanana *Niyamavali* from being destroyed."

"Did Kannappan steal the book from there?"

"It might have been risky. It was easy to tell the thieves that they were in danger."

"Then what happened?"

"They took the book from the palace and hid it elsewhere. It would be within the country. Bhimapalan somehow knew things. He discovered that the book was stolen not to destroy it, but to prevent its destruction. He hunted down and killed the thieves. He also killed Kannappan. It might have been very brutal."

There was little fear in Pappan's eyes. He asked where *Bharana Niyamavali* was hidden.

"No Idea. Those who were aware of it were killed or not. The book must be found to protect the country from danger."

"Who will find it?"

"We can also search with Serchas. We are now in the land of Thali. It is beyond time and space. Only Brahmadevananda Yogi knew the way out. If we want to know this from him, we must find *Bharana Niyamavali*."

Pappan asked, thinking about it, "Where do we look in such a vast country? Where to we start from?"

"This country has a capital. Let us begin from that point. A search for *Bharana Niyamavali*. A search for salvation."

****

Chapter 16

Ambadi indicated while taking Rishi and Pappan on a journey.

"On your way to Thali, there is a Kavu[17] near Saptadashapuram. Behind it is a mountain filled with giant trees, and there is a waterfall coming down the hill. Today is the day of full moon in the month Makaram, a day of festival. People from all over the country gather together. The festival ends with a sacrifice made in front of the Kalichan God—a human sacrifice. Choose a person who is in prison. Before the sacrifice, there is also a ceremony in which a virgin girl from the royal palace gives water to the sacrificial victim as a last rite. You can find anything useful there. Therefore, after seeing the Kalichan Kavu festival, you should visit the capital city."

He simply nodded.

---

[17]Name of devine forest

Rishi and Pappan stood outside the base of searches, ready to leave.

Pappan was on another horse. A few people participated in martial training. Some practiced horsemanship.

One man rode up to them.

"It's Manikyan," Ambadi said.

"He is one of them in Serchas. This fancy dress is intended to avoid being seen by others. There, he works as a spy in the capital city. You can share your secrets through him."

Rishi thought that was a good idea. Rishi and Pappan followed Manikyan on horseback. After crossing the forest, horses were driven slightly faster.

Manikyan shouted loudly, "We have to reach the Kavu before noon. The sacrifice is performed when the sun reaches its peak."

They rode quickly. The path led them through the middle of the arecanut plantation, then beside the fields, along the riverbank, and over gravel above the laterite rock.

Before noon, they reached the Kavu. They tied the horses to a tree and mingled with the crowd. Pappan followed Rishi, but Manikyan disappeared. Most people carried water in their hands. When Rishi asked someone from the crowd, he learned that the water came from the waterfall on the hill. People believed it was divine. This water was thought to bring longevity and good health.

As they walked, Rishi told Pappan, "Didn't I tell you that Kalichan Kavu and this hill are full of wormwood trees? Wormwood can absorb toxic particles from water, soil, and air. Maybe that's why the leaves and fruits are so bitter! The water on this land is clean and free of toxins. That is why it a source of health and longevity."

It was new knowledge to Pappan. The road was paved with stone slabs, and after every ten steps, a straight path was found. People came in crowds. Rishi and Pappan joined them. Street merchants sat along the roadsides. A hornpipe was played. Rishi with Pappan ran through the crowd, climbing the stairs. A basement had been built around the old wormwood tree, with a temporary tent made of coconut leaves. Earthen lamps surrounded the floor, decorated with garlands. A symbol was carved at the base of the wormwood tree. The image was as old as the tree itself. A lamp was lit in front of it. Rishi and Pappan could not enter because of the crowd, but they managed to squeeze through a small gap and made their way to the front. On the right side of the floor, a person sat on a stone. He was a middle-aged man with an unshaven face and unkempt hair, his eyes devoid of expression.

Pappan whispered to Rishi, "Is this the man to whom the human sacrifice is given?"

Rishi made a gesture to Pappan to keep silent.

The man, who appeared to be the priest, poured water onto the man on the pedestal from an earthen pot. Two men came and stood him up. Quietly, he stood on his knees in front of a lamp that lit in front of the holly wormwood tree.

In the midst of the commotion, Rishi noticed the trembling of an anklet. He turned his head to right and saw a girl with mesmerizing beauty and two friends approaching.

Pappan whispered, "She is the royal girl."

Her hair waved in a breeze. She carried an earthen pot on the plate and poured water from the pot into the man's hand. After taking a sip, he folded his hand towards the lamp. Chitrangana sprinkled remaining water of the earthen pot on the people gathered there. When a drop of holy water fell on Rishi's eyelid, a shiver spread through his body as if a cold spring had been poured inside. While slowly opening his eyes, she was hiding somewhere in the crowd, the princess of the Thali Kingdom.

Two men in red silk came and took the man to the altar in front of the holy lamp to offer sacrifices. One of them held a sword. The altar was located in the middle of the wormwood trees behind the Kalichan basement. The bell rang again. Drum sounds filled the air. People were not allowed to enter. When the trumpet sounded, the two men returned. Everyone waited in anticipation. As the sounds stopped, the trees began to tremble in the distance. The monkeys jumped from the trees as if frightened. The crowd fell silent.

A terrifying figure approached the altar. People held their breath. A giant bear took the sacrifice from the altar in both hands and slowly retreated into the forest. It was like silence after a great storm.

The sacrifice was the final ceremony of the Kalichan Kavu festival. People began to leave the Kavu after receiving neem leaves, flowers, and water.

Rishi looked around as if searching for someone.

"I'll be right back," he told Pappan and ran down the stairs. He then rode the horse to the north.

He thought to himself,"Who's that girl? Why did she come to me in my dreams?"

Rishi rode swiftly through the meadow on the slope of the hill. The river flowed to the right. Rishi saw her horse cart was moving like a cloud in the distance. He gripped the bridle tightly and spurred it. The distance between the horse and the cart decreased. The horse moved to the right, parallel to the cart. Rishi's eyes fixed on the cart's window. Two unblinking eyes stared back at him. They held tremendous magnetic power.

"Princess of the Thali kingdom, how did you get the bridle in your eyes to control me?"

He stopped his horse where the two paths diverged. He waited there until the horses cart had passed. A rainbow appeared in the east, just above the horse cart.

****

Chapter 17

"Welcome to Thali."

It was carved on a large stone in front of the city gate. Below it, it was also written that it was 'built by King Dharmapala.'

The name of the capital of the Thali Kingdom was Thali itself. Two towers stood on either side of the main entrance, each three stories tall. The shadows of the towers extended far west. The entrance was designed so that it could be closed with a large door.

Rishi and Pappan were surprised when they entered the capital city of Thali through the city gate. The city was beautiful, with a wide paved road. There was a footpath on both sides for pedestrians, and drainage had been constructed for sewage water. A large and beautiful garden was maintained along the road, with trees planted on both sides.

Rishi, Pappan, and Manikyan walked along the footpath on the right side of the road. A horse ran past them. A woman walked up on the sidewalk. Statues and sculptures adorned the garden.

They rested for some time at an inn on the side of the road, where free food was provided to travelers: rice soup with turmeric and chili powder.

When Rishi stood at the threshold of the verandah in front of the inn, he noticed that about ten to twelve sculptors working on a new statue next to it. Rishi approached one of the sculptors and asked him what they were making. He learned that King Bhimapalan's statue was being made. A large statue, fifty or sixty feet in height. Rishi was surprised by the depiction of Bhimapalan. "His face is full of pride," he thought. When Rishi returned to the inn, Manikyan was getting ready to leave.

Manikyan said,"It is dangerous for the three of us to walk together anymore. There is a Kalmandapu[18] with a lamp in the middle, and we can gather there when the lamp is lit in the evening."

Manikyan grabbed his bag and walked down another path starting from the public square.

Pappan came to Rishi and asked, "What is our agenda?"

"We will walk around the city until the lighting of the lamp at Kalmandap in the evening."

Pappan and Rishi walked down the street. The shadows began to lengthen.

---

[18] Small house made of stones.

Behind the trees, there was a large pond filled with white lotuses.

Two street merchants crossed them with earthen pots tied at both ends of a bamboo fence. On the other side of the road, there was a large open ground. Rishi noticed several people amidst trees: soldiers practicing martial arts. Some people were riding horses, some undergoing training, and others practicing archery on a straw-made dummy.

They continued walking down the road again.

The old banyan tree was surrounded by a basement, and a dance floor next to it. On the wall behind the stage, a picture was painted with charcoal.

Rishi thought,"King Dharmapala must have been a great promoter of art."

The front of the dance floor was a semicircular earthen platform. Kalmandapu was located there. From a distance, it resembled a small temple. The center of the room housed a stone lamp. The sloping roof was composed of layers of limestone, and each pillar was angled to withstand the wind. Steps on all four sides led to the temple.

The sun sketched the shape of Kalmandapam on the soil with its shadows.

Again, while walking on the footpath, Pappan thought about Kalmandap, which had been built without any lime or clay—a marvel of stone

The astonishment of Pappan grew when he came in front of the royal palace. It was a large palace with a courtyard, a three-story building with a verandah on each floor. At the porch, thirty-two wooden pillars were constructed with beautiful carvings.

No one suspected Rishi and Pappan as they stood with the people standing in the courtyard of the royal palace, waiting to buy paddy. By the time people started to disperse, Rishi and Pappan walked back as well.

A soldier on horseback noticed them, stopped, dismounted, and walked toward them.

"I haven't you seen here before? Who you are?"

"We are traders," they both answered simultaneously. "We are looking for jobs."

"What work do you do?"

"I will do whatever I can,"Rishi said.

"Are you ready to join the army?"

Before he could answer, he asked Pappan, "What are you doing as a trader?"

"Well ..." he began to reply.

"He is a sculptor. His occupation is to collect clay, make sculptures, and sell them," Rishi said.

"Um... You should come to the royal palace tomorrow with the sculptures you have made. You can decide your future there."

Swathwa Viprasthitha: THE VOYAGE OF SOUL

The soldier turned to Rishi."Let's move for military training…"

"Now?"

"Yes, it's the right moment."

Rishi and Pappan felt trapped.

Rishi reached at the training camp.

He stood on the mud-strewn ground of the martial arts area. Three martial training participants gathered around him. He quickly realized something was wrong. As the three prepared for a wrestling match, Rishi placed his left hand on his back and touched the ground with his right hand, bowing. He then looked at all three of them at once, crossing his hands in front of his chest, with the thumb of his right foot on the ground and his left foot raised across his chest.

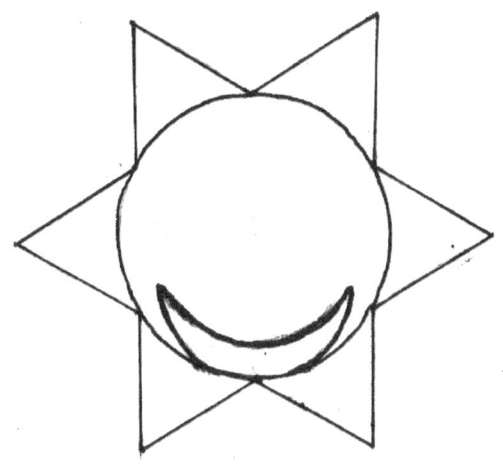

****

Chapter 18

It was a tradition in Thali Nagar that the day ended with a member of the royal family lighting the lamp at the Kalmandap in the center of the town. All work had to be completed before the lights come on. A large bell was hung near the temple. The bell rang six times, indicating that the lamp was burning.

Rishi stood on the mud-strewn ground of the martial arts area. Three martial training participants gathered around him. He quickly realized that something was wrong. As the three of them were preparing for a wrestling match, Rishi placed his left hand on the back and touched the ground with his right hand and bowed. Looking at three of them at once, he put his hands crossed in front of his chest, and with the thumb of his right foot on the ground, he raised his left foot across his chest. When Rishi was ready to wrestle with martial experts, he heard the sound of the bell.

A man approached him and said,"The day's work is over when the sound of the bell is heard. Do not do any work after that."

Rishi placed his left foot on the ground.

"To join the army of the Thali Kingdom, you must come for training from the morning itself."

Rishi looked around as if the matter wasn't clear. As everyone left, Rishi walked out.

There was a crowd in Kalmandapu: men, women, children, and the elderly. Lamps were visible in everyone's hands.

Rishi joined the crowd.

Suddenly, he realised the sound of a single anklet among the noise.

Chitrangana and two girls walked toward Kalmandap through the city street. One held a lamp in her hand, and the other carried a jar full of oil. Rishi looked at Chitrangana from head to toe. A single stone ornament hung on the forehead with her curly hair. As she walked, the bangles and the single anklet jingled. The reddish sunlight shone on her velvet dhavani. People made way for her. She climbed the narrow steps of Kalmandap, poured oil onto the lamp, and lit it from the lampstand in her hand. Her face lit up with the rays from the lamp, making her even more beautiful.

The lamp was received from Chitrangana's hand by one of the elders of the group. Light was transmitted from one lamp to another and from there to the others.

Another tradition was that the light in the houses was lit from the lampstand of Kalmandap.

After Chitrangana returned to the palace, the people dispersed.

"I'll be back soon," Rishi said, then went into the dark.

Flambeaus were lit on both sides of the city. The troops were moving around. Under the cover of darkness, Rishi walked toward the royal palace. Light shone through the windows. Girls' laughter could be heard from the third floor. He hid under the tree and watched them. Somewhere inside the palace, someone was singing on a flute. There was a large mango tree in front of the palace. A branch of the mango tree reached the verandah on the third floor. Rishi climbed to the top of the tree and ascended to the second floor. When his weight was removed, the branch of the mango tree slightly shook. He walked slowly on the roof. The girls had left by then. When he turned his face towards the breeze, Rishi saw Chitrangana behind the thin window curtain sitting on the bed with both legs placed over the bed. Rishi twisted his tongue and called out like the whistle of a cuckoo bird. Chitrangana got up from her thoughts and looked around. When the whistle was repeated, she followed the call and reached the verandah.

The shock on her face was clearly visible.

Rishi lowered his voice. "I'm here to return it. This anklet that fell on the steps of the pool... don't let the jingling anklet stay on one leg."

The wonder in Chitrangana's eyes hadn't yet faded.

Hearing footsteps below, Rishi looked into her eyes, smiled with his eyes and walked back. As he jumped to the branch, it shook noticeably. Hearing the sound, a soldier in the north courtyard looked up and saw the branch swaying slowly. Rishi stood motionless on the branch. Then, he heard a noise from the lower branch of the tree. The soldier turned around and saw a monkey jumping from the lower branch to another.

Chitrangana's cheeks turned scarlet as a smile crept across her lips from a cuckoo-like whistle that came from someplace in the shadow of the night.

****

Chapter 19

Rishi spent the entire day at the training camp. In the evening, Chitrangana did not come to light the lamp in Kalmandap. However, another lady from the palace came and lit the lamp.

Rishi and Pappan sat at the base of the banyan tree and discussed what had happened that day.

"Today I got the news from the palace, but it was a bitter one."

Rishi looked into Pappan's eyes with anxiety.

"One of the men who was assigned to steal the book *'Bharana Niyamavali'* from the palace was sacrificed at Kalichan Kavu."

Rishi felt as though a large stone had fallen in his thoughts. A bat flew nearby in the dark.

Manikyan came to Pappan and Rishi, who were waiting in the basement under the banyan tree.

"The name of the man who was making the statue of King Bhimapalan is Nakulan. His younger brother's name was Bharatan, an architect, suspect in the theft of *Bharana Niyamavali.*"

"Where does he live?"

"Who?"

"Nakulan"

"His house is on the riverbank outside the city."

Rishi looked at Pappan.

"Let's not waste time,"Pappan said.

Rishi, Pappan, and Manikyan fled the city on separate horses.

A light shone from a shed on the riverbank—a small but beautiful hut. They sat on the floor in the verandah of the hut and talked.

"We have come to know about your brother Bharatan."

At first, Nakulan kept silent. After lighting another lamp for more brightness, he began to speak.

"Bharatan made most of the sculptures in the city. He is the one among the team who built the palace. The construction of the palace is the manifestation of his full potential in Thachusasthram.Once, Bharatan was assigned to build a swinging cot for Bhimapalan. The cot had to be made of sandalwood. Bharatan built the cot within the stipulated time. However, when examining the cot, two or three planks were fake. Sandalwood perfume was applied to cheap wood. Bharatan was jailed because of his assistant's mistake."

Nakulan was silent again. "On a rainy day, when it was pouring, my brother came to our house, gave me a bag, and told me that someone would come to buy it. A man came looking for me... someone sent to save the country from danger. So far, no one has come to look for my brother or this bag."

Nakulan went inside and retrieved a bag.

"Shall we open it?"

"Of course..."

Pappan opened the bag. They found various tools, such as chisels, hatchets, and wooden hammers. A roll of leather was found between them. He took a piece of cloth and examined it. There was nothing more about it, just a picture.

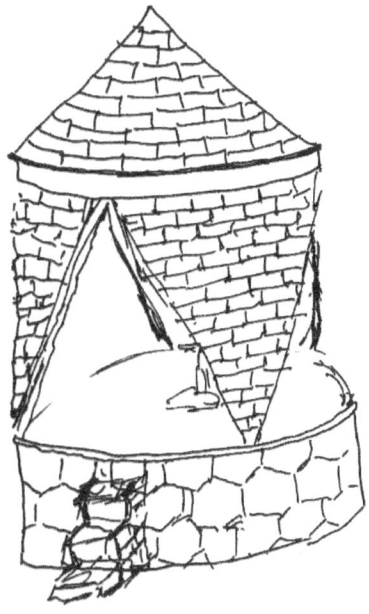

The drawing of two rings connected to each other and inscribed with letters eighteen and twelve in Malayalam numerals inside the rings. Apart from this, nothing else was written or inscribed.

The four of them looked at the picture, and the silence between them deepened.

Rishi and his friends left with the bag.

As the snow fell in the moonlight, Rishi thought while lying on sand on the river bank, "What does that picture indicate?"

Pappan also pondered the same thing. Rishi fell asleep at some point during the night. In the early morning, he woke up as he heard the sound of birds. He called Pappan. Only twilight in the sky. They took baths from the river. Pappan talked as they walked back from the river.

"I don't remember seeing a picture like this anywhere...?"

"What if the geography of this city resembles that picture?"

"Then what about the numbers?"

"Now we have to check if there are any symbols in the city that denote eighteen and twelve."

Suddenly, Rishi stopped. The twilight rays fell on his face. He closed his eyes and visualized the pictures in his mind.

He asked to Pappan, "Can you tell me what that picture was?"

"Two rings"

Without opening his eyes, Rishi said calmly.

Pappan opened the piece of leather in his hand.

"The two interlinked circles, with twelve and eighteen written on each circle."

A smile spread across Rishi's lips.

"Two different human beings are connected...?"

Pappan's eyes widened. "In marriage?"

"Of course... In the case of Bharatan, these two circles may represent the father and the mother. And twelve and eighteen mean the parents were from the villages Dwadashapura or Ashtadashapura."

They immediately returned to Nakulan's house and spoke to him.

Nakulan said, "Yes, our mother's house is in Ashtadashapuram, and our father's house is in Dwadashapuram."

Rishi looked at Pappan and smiled.

'Bharathan, who is in jail, has been entrusted with the task of stealing the Bharana Niyamavali. Along with Bharathan, another prisoner was also appointed. Not only to steal the book but also to destroy it. Bharathan realised that it was the biggest treason. Bharathan stole the book and hid it somewhere else. A secret code was also prepared to be useful for whoever came to find it. Convinced that he would be killed, Bharathan surrendered the secret to Nakula and went into hiding. King Bhimapala sends a man to find and kill Bharathan.'

Rishi thought the brilliance of Bharathan.

The morning lightbathed them all.

****

Chapter 20

"Today I took off the anklet," Chitrangana said to Rishi. "The black mole on your ankle is more beautiful when you wear anklets."

A little house beyond the northern courtyard of the palace was made of bamboo and covered with hay and grass. It was a place for women during their menstrual period.

Sitting by the side of a bamboo wall, Chitrangana spoke to Rishi. He sat on the opposite side of the wall. Rishi used to meet Chitrangana secretly in the palace. They talked until the early hours of night. A gentle breeze swept over them. They were still talking in the moonlight.

"I have to leave in the morning," Rishi said.

"Where?"

"For a long distance. There's a lot of work to be done."

"When are you coming back?"

"I don't know, not for a long time. The moonlight is gone. Let me go... "

"A little later please..."

Moonlight scattered inside the house. Chitrangana said, drawing her nails on the cow dung-waxed floor, "I have a doubt. Shall I ask?"

"What?"

"I don't know if I love you…"

A light breeze caught him there.

Rishi was confused and thought about it, "I love her back. But is that possible? What will be the end? Will this be meaningless love?"

Rishi asked, "Do you know what love is?"

"Eh! Why did you ask?"

"Nothing, let me tell you a story..."

Rishi remained silent for some time and then said, "This is Parvathi's story."

"A graveyard. Parvathi sat under the gulmohar tree, recalling something while combing her hair. Dresses were spread out.

Pain covered her body. However, the smile near her dimple indicated that the pain had a beautiful feeling. She rose from among the fallen gulmohar flowers. She placed a red flower in her hair. The Sun had not yet begun to shine. Snow waited for the sun to melt. It was then that Parvathi saw Lord Shiva sitting on the rock outside the graveyard. There, among the rocks, a yellow bellflower was also blossoming."

"Shiva heard the sound of anklets coming closer through the fog."

"Parvathi kissed Shiva's forehead from behind, hugged him, and caressed his hair with her left hand. Shiva looked at her. The bindi on her forehead had disappeared. A smile of gratitude hung at the corner of her eye, indicating gratitude for providing beautiful sex."

"Lord Shiva suddenly turned around and looked away. There was something sad in his mind. Parvathi sensed this and said, 'I am your Sathi. The same love, your love.'"

"A cool breeze blew across Shiva's face. Lord Shiva looked into Parvati's eyes. When Parvati's eyesight faded, she realized that both of her eyes were full. Parvathi said, rubbing her hard chest with her cheeks, 'I'll always be here. And I was right here.'"

"Shiva felt relaxed. He hugged her tightly. The red gulmohar flowers were falling."

Rishi had closed his eyes, listening to the sounds of the night. Moonlight was just beginning to fade. His eyes were filled.

Rishi asked, listening to the voice of sigh, "Are you crying?

"I don't know why I am crying."

Both of them remained silent for a long time. They did not speak to each other until the night ended.

****

Chapter 21

In the morning, while riding on the horse, the glow of the moonlight remained inside Rishi. Manikyan, Pappan, and Rishi were located at the edge of the forest. It took a long time for sunrays to reach beyond mountains.

Manikyan said, "This is Chekkikunnu hills. It is a steep climb, and Ashtadasapuram is beyond this hill. We can't ride horses anymore here. Let me tie the horses somewhere."

They made their way up a steep hillside through a narrow path lined with bushes, small trees, vines, and pebbles. The sunlight began to spread. They climbed the hill, holding onto the Kadamba vines to prevent slipping, and finally reached the top.

The three of them looked to the east. Their faces become dry as no green could be seen in front of them.

Manikyan said softly, "There were a lot of trees, a place where the carpenters lived. Their primary occupations were carpentry and agriculture."

In front of them were torn, dry fields, and dry trees standing with only twigs, without leaves. Pappan and Rishi looked at each other. They went down to the deserted land. In contrast, women climbed the hill with empty pots to fetch water. Rishi, Pappan, and Manikyan walked through the middle of the dry field and reached a crowded place. The skin and faces of many people were pale and wrinkled. Their lips and eyelids were dry. As Pappan was preparing to ask an old man lying on a rope bed in front of a hut, Rishi held Pappan's hand and gestured no.

"It's not the right time... let's go and watch here. Come..."

They walked across the villages. There were no fences or boundary walls. Upon reaching a house, they saw people running in a panic. One of them was stopped and asked by Manikyan.

"Virundan's hut caught fire... even though his wife and child were inside it."

Before he could finish, the man ran, followed by Rishi, Pappan, and Manikyan.

The fire, which had started in the kitchen due to wind, spread all over the hut.

Virundan sat in mud and cried loudly. Some people threw sand and gravel onto the hut. Rishi shouted, "Is there any water here?"

No one listened to his words. Some stared at him blankly. As they could find nothing else, Rishi and his friends threw sand on the roof. Some women ran with pots of water. As they tried to put out the fire, Rishi saw a figure covered in flames crawling out of the hut. Everyone stood still. As the figure crawled into the courtyard, Virundan called out, "Vellachee," and leaped over to her. Some people stopped and hugged him.

Rishi took a pot from the hands of those who came with water and poured it over the figure. When the fire was put out, Virundan collapsed onto her with a loud voice, clasping her with both hands. It was Vellachi, Virundan's wife. Everyone was shocked to find her infant child under her, held tightly to her chest to protect him from fire. Rishi pulled the baby out from Vellachi. The baby's heartbeat stopped. He laid the baby on the floor and pressed his hand on his chest five times. Rishi closed the baby's mouth and blew through it. The same procedure was repeated. The baby woke up for the third time, crying. The child had injuries to the head and hands.

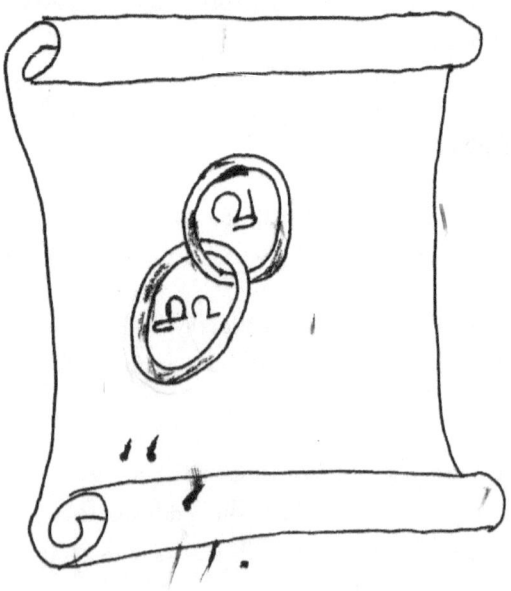

The remaining water was poured on the ground, and mud was created. Rishi applied the mud all over the body of the baby. Suddenly, a loud cry erupted from Virundan, turning into a collective wail. Vellachi died because most parts of her body were burned. A woman came and took the baby. The fire was finally extinguished, and only smoke rose from the ashes.

The pyre burned on the hillside near a leafless wormwood tree. Above it, there was a dry silence. Rishi, Pappan, and Manikyan stood nearby. The people began to return. Only Virundan and a woman with the baby remained.

"It is customary to cremate a person who dies in an accident like this."

"What if it is a natural death?" Pappan asked doubtfully. Manikyan explained, "If it is a normal death, they bury the body in an urn called Nannangadi... There's a village meeting tonight to discuss what happened here, an emergency meeting. We should attend it."

"Yes," Rishi whispered.

There was nothing but darkness ahead. Rishi became silent after the incident. Villagers gathered around the fire. Rishi, Pappan, and Manikyan sat on the verandah of a nearby house and listened to conversations. One person began talking about the tragedy that had occurred there.

"I will tell you about the incidents that happened here before today's tragedy. A few weeks ago, Ambu's daughter, Umbichi, died from vomiting and diarrhea. The Vaidyar said it was due to drinking contaminated water. Every afternoon, a hot storm occurred here. It was such a wind that a branch from the jackfruit tree fell on Kottan's house. In the absence of water, the crops were destroyed. All the grass in the field was burned. Many people are suffering from various health problems. Therefore, we need a solution to these problems."

The village chief remained silent and did not answer.

Another person stood and said, "We have to leave this place.

"Leaving this land? This is the land where our ancestors lived."

Another voice from the crowd said, "That was true. They were alive. However, we struggle to live here. Beyond this hill is a lush, green area with abundant water. Let's move our lives there."

"If we find a solution for water here, won't all the problems end?" someone asked.

Everyone fell silent. No one spoke. Rishi got up and walked toward the hill, followed by Pappan and Manikyan. They sat on the rock.

Rishi said,"This village is the soul of the people who live here. They don't want to leave. But the situation is forcing them to leave."

"So, what will we do? Have we come here to gather any proof of the *Bharana Niyamavali*?"

"Wait, the opportunity will come."

Due to the long travel and that day's events, sleep had thickened the eyelids. The rooster crowded at a distance.

Before Pappan and Manikyan woke up, Rishi got up and walked through the hill. There was a lone Ezhilampala tree. He reached near the tree. Remnants of wormwood trees stood as memorials to the fallen. They were stumps of wormwood trees, from whichbeads had come out. He could hardly believe it. It was like finding happiness within.

He went down the hill and reached the field. He ran through the fields and came to the village meeting place where the meeting had been held the previous day. He grabbed the rope tied to the bell on the tree and pulled it several times. The sound of the chime startled many. The village chief came out of the house.

"I have to say one thing." Rishi said.

There was anger and disappointment with the village chief.

Pappan and Manikyan had reached there by then.

Rishi looked around, and people gathered.

"Your problems will be solved. We will bring the water as you need."

He looked Pappan, surprise in his eyes.

"If you give a few people who will work hard, we can start the work of getting water today itself."

The village chief walked slowly in front of Rishi and asked him to place both hands on his shoulder."Is this true?"

He paused and looked around to say, "The entire village will be with you."

The village chief hugged and embraced Rishi. He said to those who were there, "You must come to the slope of the hill. Take the spade, hoe, spear, and vine basket in your hand."

The sunbeam began to heat up. Rishi said this as he walked with Pappan, "I was walking on the hilltop when I saw a tree, Ezhilampala. In some places, it is called the Milkwood tree. There is a greater possibility of waterlogging in the presence of an Ezhilampala. There were many wormwood-tree stumps in the vicinity. New buds were emerging from it. There is no doubt about the presence of water. I have heard it being said that Athirani plants grow in the presence of clean water. There is a lot of this in the area. There is plenty of water in the mountain."

"Why is there no water in the village? The village is near the mountain."

"I'll explain. Look at this hill and its slope. It slopes from north to south. Most likely, the water flows from north to south. The village is located on the eastern side of a mountain. Prior to this, it was a forest. There were many trees. Still, if you dig into the soil, you can see the roots buried in the ground as the remnants of the forest. The roots of the trees allowed water to flow from the hill to the village. However, there are currently no trees. This is the reason for the drought."

They sat under a neem tree in the middle of the paddy field. The enthusiasm of Pappan had grown.

Swathwa Viprasthitha: THE VOYAGE OF SOUL

"Delivering the water from the hill to the villagers... that is possible if we try. The tunnel was made horizontal to the hill, as well as to the flow of water. Water seeped from the hill into the tunnel. This water should be brought to the pond, which will be made on the slope of the hill. Of course, if the villagers make collective efforts, they will be able to fetch water without any delay."

The shadow of the neem tree grew shorter.

The villagers walked through the embankments of the fields to the hill slope. They included women, children, and the elderly. The sky was clear, and blue clouds were observed in the sky. Pappan created groups of people there. Each group was assigned different duties. One group dug the tunnel, another group moved of earth, and another group dug the pond near the slope of the hill. Meanwhile, some women turned themselves into another group for preparing food.

Pappan provided exact measurements for people digging the tunnel. Everyone worked hard. The sun set that day unwillingly. The work of the tunnel moved very slowly due to the hard rock. With everyone's enthusiasm, the pond work was almost complete. The sun was up early for the next eight days to see Ashtadasapura's natives. On the ninth day, the sun rose to witness something.

When the villagers reached the tunnel in the morning, they saw water flowing out of it. It flowed like a waterfall into the lake. The villagers were happy and overjoyed. They danced, laughed, and cried with joy. Some people came and carried Rishi and Pappan on their shoulders. It was a festival throughout the village. All of them gathered at the meeting site.

Village chief asked, "This is the request of the village. And what do we have to offer you in return? I know it is not enough, but what do you want? You can ask."

He stood up and looked at the people sitting quietly.

"'Karmanyevadhikarastu maa phaleshu kadachana.' That means do not work expecting results. However, I am going to ask you here for the reward. In this village, many rainforest trees are planted. There were many large trees. The trees were uprooted, and the rain stopped. The roots of the tree hold back rainwater. When the trees were cut, the earth became dry. There should no longer be such droughts. So, this is my request to you."

Rishi bowed before them."Don't give up."

All the people got up from their seats. The village chief held both hands of Rishi. His eyes were full of tears—the sign of acceptance of Rishi's request

After the meeting, everyone left. Only the village chief, Rishi, Pappan, and Manikyan were left. Then, Rishi asked, "We need to tell you something."

"Tell me."

"Bharatan…"

The name shocked the village head.

"He is my nephew… Where is he?"

"We don't know where he is at the moment. But it is certain that he has made a great sacrifice to save the entire country. A great sacrifice."

The village chief thoroughly looked at all three men. He then went to home. When he returned, he had a wooden box in his hand. He handed the box to Rishi.

"My child told me this. 'Someone will come looking for it for the kingdom of Thali. Gave it to them.'"

Rishi and Pappan were amazed at Bharatan's foresight.

The box opened. It was round and made of wood. There was nothing else. Pappan took that shape in his hand and thoroughly examined it.

Rishi said in his mind, "Next to Dwadashapuram."

****

Chapter 22

The river was wide. The boatman asked Rishi, Pappan, and Manikyan while crossing the river in a boat, "Where are you from? Are you going to Chenan's house?"

Pappan and Rishi looked at each other. They had come to Ashtadashapura in search of Bharatan's father's house.

"He was bedridden for a long time. Last night, he vomited thick amounts of blood. With that, he passed away."

Pappan asked with confusion, "Who is Chenan?"

The boatman asked, holding on to the oar. "He is the headman of carpenters' family at this area. Who to see are you going there?"

"Isn't this Bharatan's house?"

"Which Bharatan? The famous carpenter, isn't he?"

"Yes... yes."

"Chenan is his grandfather. Anyway, you'll be there soon. Let's see before the body is taken."

People had gathered around the house in the middle of the aracanut garden. Walking through the ridge of the garden and climbing the steps, they reached the front of the house. An old man approached them and said, "The body has just been taken from here."

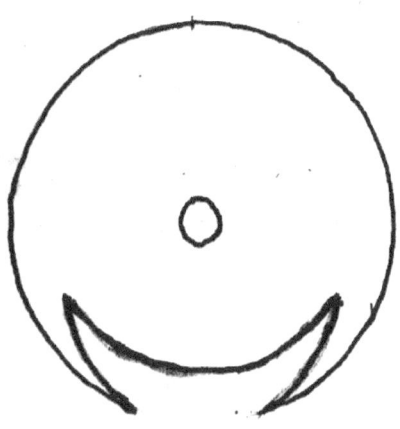

Pappan interjected, "No problem."

Rishi, Pappan, and Manikyan stood there for a while and then walked down through the garden.

On the third day, they came back. There were fewer people. Rishi entrusted Manikyan to inquire about Bharatan. When Manikyan entered the house and spoke to the elderly, Rishi and Pappan stood near the well. The children were playing beside the well.

When Manikyan returned, there was a slight disappointment on his face.

Following Manikyan, Nakulan also arrived.

"Why are you here?" he asked.

"According to the instructions of Bharata, from Ashtadashpuram and Dwadashpuram, any evidence may be obtained about the book Bharana Niyamavali. Evidence was obtained from Dwadashapura. The rest part may be obtained from here."

"It's been a long time since Bharatan visited here. No one knows anything about him. And if anything was handed over to anyone, it must have been Chenan, his grandfather."

He closed his eyes. His thoughts became empty.

They descended the stone steps and walked through the areca nut garden. Among the children, one pulled the other child on the arecanut palm. While watching the children's play, an object caught Rishi's eyes. A wooden box, covered with soil, similar to the box found in Ashtapuram. He quickly picked up the box. The soil was removed and the box was opened, but the interior was empty. Rishi, Pappan, and Manikyan began searching the area. Two other children played in the mud, making snacks with clay. Pappan obtained a figure made of wood from children.

The figure received from Ashtadasapura and the figure in the hands of Pappan were carved from the same wood. Pappan gave it to Rishi. Sitting on a treehouse by the bank of the river,

Swathwa Viprasthitha: THE VOYAGE OF SOUL

they closely examined the two figures. The first was large, and the second was small.

"I couldn't find what this means."

Pappan took the second figure in his hand and examined all sides. He said, "I have seen such shapes in the city. All four walls of the Kalmandapu are in this style. There is a picture on the wall behind the stage. It's this shape."

Rishi nodded, "Then what is the significance of this first figure? There is no possibility to hide such a big secret in the city. It could be somewhere outside the city."

A bamboo houseboat moved on the river.

Rishi took both the figures in his hands and examined them. On the sides of the first figure, there were about six holes. Rishi also examined the second figure. The second figure has a small tail. The hole in the first figure was such that the tail of the second figure was exactly suited. All six holes were the same size.

Pappan noticed the glint in Rishi's eyes.

Rishi showed Pappan the small figure in his hand and said, "We need to make five more figures of the same shape and size. What is the solution?

"I will do it," Manikyan said.

By the time a snake swallowed a nearby frog, rested, and crawled into its ditch, Manikyan had returned. He had made five figures, as requested by Rishi. Rishi took the figures in his hand and attached them to the holes on the sides of the first figure. When all came together, they took a different form. A new figure.

Pappan tried to recall something. He walked here and there, biting his fingernail.

"This... I have seen this form before. But where?

Rishi said, "In KalichanKavu"

"Yes, at Kalichan Kavu... at the basement of the holy wormwood tree. But..."

"Um, what?"

There were some doubts in Pappan's mind.

"Kalichan Kavu was a place where people gathered once a year. This was why *Bharana Niyamavali* was hidden somewhere safe there. Anyway, let us find it."

The birds were flying, andthe entire western horizon hadturned red.

****

Chapter 23

The whoosh sound passed through the darkness. It was followed by the sound of the piercing metal in the flesh. It was a dark room. There was only one beam of light coming in from the small window.

The sweat dripped from the heavy body to the floor. He took a bow in his left hand and aimed at the darkness in front of him. It was Bhimapalan who pulled the bowstring as far as possible and shot an arrow.

A soldier came in there. Bhimapalan tilted his head and asked, "What?"

"A street merchant, Kireedi, is waiting to meet you." Soldier replied.

Kireedi was actually one of the secret agents of Bhimapalan.Bhimapala waved his right hand for permission for Kireedi to enter.A man entered the room through the curtain.

Bhimapalan stretched the bowstring again and aimed in the darkness.

"After Bharatan, three men. They visited Ashtadasapuram and Dwadashapuram."

Bhimapalan took the next arrow and placed it on the bowstring. He said, "Follow them and know their intentions. If they are behind the book, don't make any hurdles until they find it. When they find a place where the book *Bharana Niyamavali* is located, they must be killed."

The next shot flew off in the dark.

When he stepped out of the room, someone moved the curtains on both sides. The light behind the door was turned on. As darkness fell on both sides, a man's body was found hanging from the rope. The whole body was wounded with arrows. The blood still oozed from the corner of his mouth.

****

Chapter 24

After letting Manikyan reach serchas, Rishi and Pappan went to Kalichan Kavu. It took half a day to arrive.

All the leaves and fruits had fallen on the rocksteps of the holy wormwood tree. Small bushes grew around the tree. Rishi took the figure made by Bharatan from the bag on his shoulder and placed it on the base of wormwood tree. The same shape was carved on the base of the wood. However, they had no idea about the hole in the middle. Rishi and Pappan looked around thoroughly, but no results were observed. They then returned to the tree. Pappan took the figure in his hand and looked around through the hole in the middle of it. An object passed over Pappan's head. When he looked up, the branches were moving. It might have been monkeys hanging from the trees.

Rishi searched around.

"Let's look for any indication." Pappan said, holding the figure in his palm.

"What if this hole sometimes refers to a well?"

Rishi's mind turned in another direction. He took the figure and held it perpendicular.

"This hole may indicate a cave. Yes, there is a cave right next to the altar. A cave that no one has entered."

Rishi and Pappan got up from the base and walked toward the altar. The remains of the festival were still present. Blood stains were stuck to the rocks. The snake skin lay near the burial site.

Rishi walked into the cave; dry leaves crunched under his feet. Three stone slabs placed in front of the door. They tried hard to remove them. When Rishi entered the cave, he felt darkness and moisture. He felt cold on his feet and stood motionless. A reptile crawled over his feet. By that time, Pappan had taken the shield hanging near the holy wormwood tree. This reflected sunlight toward the cave. Light flickered across the cave wall in the dark. When a stone protruded from a wall, it stuck to his hand. Rishi stood there and tried to turn it. When it turned, a door opened. He realized it was a small chamber. Rishi put his hand inside and took an object wrapped in cloth—a book wrapped in leather. The words *BHARANA NIYAMAVALI* were written on it. He came out of the cave.

Excitement and curiosity rested on Pappan's face. Rishi replied, "Here is the *BHARANA NIYAMAVALI* in my hand. With this, the anarchy of the country is going to end."

Pappan took the book from Rishi and looked around, his face filled with surprise and joy. Some monkeys jumped through the trees. Birds were flying. Rishi sensed some indication of danger.

"We won't stay here anymore. We've got to get out of here quickly."

A whooshing arrow passed between Rishi and Pappan and struck a nearby tree before Rishi could say another word. Ten or more soldiers ran towards them before the vibration of the arrow ended. Two of them had swords and daggers in their hands, while the others had bows and arrows. Not only did Rishi gave Pappan the book, he also took the shield from Pappan's hand and skillfully stopped the sword. The sword fell from the soldier's hand as Rishi kicked his shoulder.

Rishi grabbed the sword before the second soldier could attack. He ordered Pappan to move in a different direction during the battle with soldiers. The soldier with the bow shot an arrow at Pappan, but he dodged it. Then, a militant who came flying at lightning speed from above took the book from Pappan's hands.

When Pappan looked up, several figures were hanging from vines, flying from tree to tree. Pappan swung himself onto one of the vines and chased them. By the time Pappan reached from one tree to another, all soldiers had come out of Kalichan Kavu. Those who had been fighting Rishi also climbed down the steps to leave Kavu. When Rishi reached Pappan, he learned that the book had been lost. They ran through the wood behind the soldiers. A squawking falcon flew over the forest.

When Rishi exited Kalichan Kavu, he saw soldiers who had been fighting him, lying down with arrows in their chest. The other soldiers stood steady, the sharp edge of the sword at their necks. They were surrounded by Serchas. Rishi saw that the book *'BharanaNiyamavali'* was in the hands of Ambadi, safe in his possession.

****

Chapter 25

That night, all the Serchas gathered secretly in a cave near the rocks. Rishi and Pappan were with him. *Bharana Niyamavali* was a gift; what was next? That was the topic of discussion.

Their conversations continued late into the night, and the nightjar birds cried. They sat around the book, *Bharana Niyamavali*, speaking in the light of flambeaus. Ambadi, the head of the Serchas, asked each person's opinion. From a distance, jackal howls could be heard. Rishi and Pappan sat separately on a rock. Ambadi looked at Rishi and asked him, "What's your opinion?"

When Rishi looked around, everyone's eyes struck him. He got up, walked over to the book, and replied, "I feel extremely grateful and honored that Brahmadevananda has written this book. He said that governance was not just about fighting wars. It is something that should permeate every aspect of human life. For example, in this book about agriculture, at what time to cultivate, how to irrigate the farm properly, how to collect the crops, how to help distressed people, etc., are being discussed at the micro level."

"Similarly, it discusses trade, hospitality, sanitation, public works, education, law, and order in detail. Therefore, good governance is required. The lack of it is also the reason for the chaos seen today. The rulers were afraid of the trial. They were afraid of the *Bharana Niyamavali.* Therefore, the book has been kept away from the public. It should reach the people. Let people understand what is laid down in the constitution, what good governance is, and how it can be implemented."

"The book discusses the democratic method of electing a person as the king if good governance changes in the country and anarchy crops up. Therefore, people must be aware of these rules. There are eighteen villages in this country. In every village from the north to here, people should be made aware of the *Bharana Niyamavali.* Some Serchas should be held responsible. Simultaneously, it must be strengthened to deal with the existing palace army. It has to come from villages. If people move against the dictatorship as a whole, the current ruler will no longer be able to resist. Sometimes this may take a long time. But if you don't have weapons before you go to war, it will be a mistake."

There was twilight somewhere in the east. A cold wind blew, and Rishi stopped talking and walked back. There was some time left for sunrise. The birds began to fly. Serchas were dispersed from there. Rishi and Pappan were sitting quietly on the rock. The half-moon hung in the western horizon.

"What is our plan? How do we get back from here?" Pappan was worried.

"And that's what I'm thinking about. When the light spread out, I had to go somewhere—to find the answer for this."

They looked at nature and were awakened from the night.

****

Chapter 26

Rishi ventured into the woods to find Brahmadevananda. There were numerous locations where gulmohar flowers had spread. In his mind, love may have blossomed. It was Chitrangana, Rishi recalled. He ascended the slope and arrived close to the cave. Greenery covered the entire front of the cave. He shouted loudly, then he turned around and climbed up the rock behind the cave. However, beyond the veil of the mist, only the echo returned. No signs of Brahmadevananda were observed.

Then, a piece of white fabric landed on Rishi's shoulder, slipping in the breeze. He picked it up in shock. The scent was the same as that of Brahmadevananda Yogi. Rishi lost his control. The wayout would not be revealed if he is not founded.

Does Brahmadevanandayogi no longer exist? All that remains is his creation. The purpose of Brahmadevananda yogi was to save the country. The *Bharana Niyamavali* must be restored. This is what he needed him for.

Rishi strolled back through the jungle after tossing that clothing into the air. Until he exited from the forest, his mind was blank.

"What ought we to do now? Where can additional support be found? Are we stranded here?"

His mind raced with these thoughts. While returning to the horse, Rishi stopped at a place where the road was divided. One route was to the royal palace, to Chitrangana. Rishi rode the horse very quickly down that road.

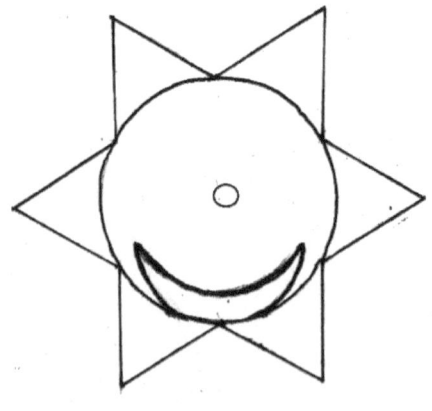

****

Chapter 27

Blood seeped from the royal sword. King Bhimapalan tremored in rage as he sat on a pedestal and held his sword to the ground. The corpses were lying in front of the throne. The other two warriors bled through their throat wounds. It was them who informed the king that the '*Bharana Niyamavali*' had been taken away by the Serchas. King Bhimapala was so afraid of '*Bharana Niyamavali*.' Walking to and fro in the middle of the palace, he flung the sword to the ground and screamed,

"Kill them. There will not be any single member in Sercha's family. Their families should be destroyed. In any case, the *Bharana Niyamavali* must be seized."

Each soldier who was present, was terrified. When Bhimapalan yelled once again, they said,

"Order!"

The rage inside him was blazing and palpable.

****

Chapter 28

"There is a land with no sound, no light, no wind, no rain, no mist, no water. When we leave our body, we reach it. I wish to be there, where not even the throbbing sound of a heartbeat or the sound of a breath exists. That is the better place to cherish your memories."

Rishi said sitting on a branch of a mango tree in the northern courtyard of the palace. Rishi's words reached Chitrangana's ears through the coconut shell, then through the stretched thread connecting two shells, and again another coconut shell at the other end. Remote talk is possible through there.

Chitrangana sat on the verandah on the third floor. She asked, "What are you talking about?"

"That's real. We truly love each other. Because of this, our love will last even in the absence of a body."

"Please don't talk to me like that."

The thread between Rishi and Chitrangana was sometimes silent.

Like a wave, Chitrangana's ruckle made its way to Rishi.

"Chitrangana, as I told you earlier, we are two different truths. I am from a different land, a different time. Actually, I should not have loved you, but I do not know what the end will be. Sometimes, love between us can lock me up here. If this is true.."

A cold breeze blew through.

A soldier, watching Chitrangana's movements, secretly whispered something to another soldier. Rishi was not visible to him.

Again, silence wandered between Rishi and Chitrangana.

The second soldier sneaked through the roof above the third floor and moved towards Chitrangana without her knowledge. As he approached her, he heard her speaking. He realized there was a thread running from her to the mango tree.

Unbeknownst to Chitrangana, he poured lamp oil onto the thread and lit it. Rishi saw the fire on the thread. Before he could do anything else, Rishi saw ten or more soldiers coming with weapons at the foot of the mango tree.

Two soldiers also came to Chitrangana. Rishi had no other choice; he jumped from the top of the tree to the ground. The soldiers surrounded him with the weapons.

By then, the mango tree had been engulfed in flames.

****

Chapter 29

Chitrangana was lying down on a silk carpet spread on the floor. She was whining. There were injury marks on her body, and the blood oozed from her nose. The king, Bhimapalan, sat in a nearby hanging chair. He sat as he held her left hand in a chain and crossing his right leg over the other. There was anger in his eyes.

The lights from the lamps in the room were flickered by wind.

Chitrangana's mother, Gauri, was standing in front of King Bhimapalan.

Chitrangana was considered to be the bride of Bhimapalan from childhood. However, she did not like him. She made several attempts to escape the marriage. Once, she danced alone in a public in the city. She continued without stopping. She was in a frenzy. People from the palace came and took her back. This continued many times and in many places. It was an escape from marriage. The palace physician was Chitrangana's favorite. He identified it as a mental illness. He said that the treatment would last for at least three years. Thus, Chitrangana escaped marriage for some time.

Chitrangana lifted her head and looked at a sword's swoosh sound. Blood was splashed on her face. Nearby, the physician fell down and screamed. The sword was nailed to his chest.

"Tomorrow morning there will be a wedding tent in front of the palace."

King Bhimapalan's voice resounded in the palace.

"The next day is King Bhimapalan's wedding. The palace will stand witness; the people here will stand witness; and this country will witness. Chitrangana will become King Bhimapalan's wife."

It was a terrible sound.

****

Chapter 30

One of the Serchas stood at the top of a high rock, looking around. He saw a soldier riding a horse towards the rocks in the dark, and he ran into the cave.

"The army of the palace has reached our cave."

All the serchas became alert, took out their weapons and ran out of the cave. The man who had come on the horseback let out a special whistle by pressing his lips.

Ambadi came forward, raised his left hand, and gestured to Serchas.

"He is our man. One of the soldiers of the palace who works for us."

Ambadi inquired,"What is the matter? Anything unusual?"

Marathan provided information about Rishi's arrests. Everyone was shocked to hear this.

"Why did he go there?"

Marathan replied, "The evidence was ambiguous. His affair with Princess Chitrangana is the reason for his incarceration. It is also known that King Bhimapalan and Princess Chitrangana are marrying the next day."

Ambadi gave a look to Pappan. Pappan was stunned by the news. Serchas were preoccupied with the idea of rescuing Rishi. Nobody had a precise response.

"Since we are a small group, fighting the palace army will be risky for us," Ambadi continued. "However, this will not be considered."

One of them says loudly, "We need to grow our team."

"We have no time for this."

"Just try."

When Pappan heard the discussion, he ascended the rock. From the top, he looked toward the palace. The light of the half-moon was apparent in the sky.

****

Chapter 31

A prison that was dark. The whip caused blood to drip from the wound. Rishi attempted to sit up by pressing his right hand against the floor. The entire body hurt. He was alone in a prison cell.

"Who are you?"

The voice came from an adjacent cell. Rishi had no intention of responding. The inquiry carried immense authority, and he soon recognized the voice. A reasonable individual would not ask such a question. Rishi got a sense that he was in a position of authority. He guessed that King Vijayapala might be the owner of the voice.

"I am Rishi; it's not important. I've heard a lot about you. You're the king Vijayapalan, right?"

"I am not the king of anybody."

"Sorry, I didn't mean that. I played a small part in the mission of getting you out of this prison. Most importantly, the *Bharana Niyamavali* was recovered. That was my task, and I completed it. The book is now in the hands of the Serchas. They will end the prevailing anarchy in the country with the help of the public. And you will be released."

"Is that true?"

"Yes, it's true, but it's hard to say how long it will take for people's march."

Rishi heard the sound of two feet moving. There was no more conversation, only silence.

He sat on the ground with his legs crossed, closed his eyes, concentrated his mind, and merged in meditation.

****

Chapter 32

The first rays of the sun fell on the wedding tent built in front of the palace. Beads were used to embellish each wall. The wedding stage was filled with a variety of flowers. Two elephants in caparison stood at the entrance. With the exception of the wedding stage, many stages were set up. On one stage, some troupes were singing, while others were dancing. People began to flow toward the palace.

King Bhimapalan's marriage.

The people assembled rose when Bhimapalan, clad in gaudy clothing, and wearing a turban, entered the tent with his warriors. The ritual hearth, set up on the stage, emitted a scent of sandalwood and ghee.

After Bhimapalan, two soldiers brought Rishi into the chains and dragged him to the tent. Injury marks and blood stains were visible on his body. They tied Rishi to the tent's main pillar. People gasped at the sight.

Rishi tried to open his eyelids. The wedding stage was seen. King Bhimapalan was seated on a pedestal behind the ritual hearth.

The girls and women made a melodious chorus. Chitrangana walked behind an old lady holding a lit lamp. Seven beautiful girls followed her. They walked toward the stage and circled the ritual hearth. Chitrangana's eyes were filled with tears.

She had blurry vision. Chitrangana was made to sit behind the ceremonial hearth.

Chitrangana was disturbed by the sounds of nadaswaram, chenda, and other musical instruments. She leaned forward and held her right hand to hold her head. All she could think of was Rishi. She opened her eyes when someone patted her. In front of her, king of Bhimapalan was holding a garland of flowers. An elderly woman presented to Chitrangana another garland. Bhimapalan grinned at Chitrangana. At the corners of his mouth hung a sneer.

Looking at Rishi, he said, "Special witness is present at our wedding. Look at that."

Chitrangana glanced toward the hall.

"This is his last vision."

She shut and opened her eyes to clear her vision and looked at him in shock. Rishi was tied to a pole.

"No, this marriage should not happen. I offered him myself. I need to be with him forever."

Seeing Chitrangana's lips whispering something, Bhimapalan asked loudly,"What...?"

"If I get married, it will be only to him."

The singers and dancers suddenly ceased. The melodious chorus stopped. People stared at Chitrangana.

Chitrangana came out of the wedding stage with the garland in her hand and ran toward Rishi.

In a fit of rage, Bhimapalan threw the garland in his hand into the ritual hearth, pulled the dagger from a sheath at the waist of a soldier standing nearby, and threw it at Chitrangana. She reached Rishi with the garland, but the dagger hit Chitrangana on the back of her neck. Blood trickled down her forehead and chin. The voice did not come out of her. Chitrangana fell onto Rishi's chest. The garland draped around his neck before her demise.

He cried out, feeling helpless. He struggled to escape his handcuffs. Tears gushed from his eyes. Rishi sobbed as he kissed Chitrangana's forehead.

The crowd panicked and fled. The uncontrolled elephant ran through the people. Bhimapalan walked towards Rishi with a sword in his hand.

On the street outside the tent, Pappan waited with a chariot locked with four horses. A strong rope tied to the main pole of the tent was tightened. By the time King Bhimapalan approached Rishi, the tent had collapsed with a loud noise. As soon as Serchas came and pulled out Rishi and untied him.

Still, Chitrangana's body lied on Rishi's chest. He carried her to his left shoulder and went out.

By the time King Bhimapalan emerged from under the tent after knocking down all obstacles, the horse cart that locked the four horses had reached far away.

****

Chapter 33

On the hillside, near Kalichan Kavu, Pappan assembled twigs and tree branches to form a pyre. Chitrangana's body rested on Rishi's lap as he used his palms to close her eyelids. He still had tears in his eyes. Melancholy expression on his face.

"But if I return, it will be taken, your love. I know no one can take anything back from here."In his thoughts, he muttered it.

It was supposed to rain. There was a fierce wind coming from the south.

Chitrangana's body was placed on the pyre and set alight. The fire was fanned by the wind. As the rain intensified, the sun hid behind the clouds.

"At here, is this the ritual? Is this how bodies are cremated in this land?" Pappan asked.

"We have witnessed this before. In the case of unnatural death, the body is cremated by fire. If it is a natural death, it is buried in a pot named 'Chara.'"

"Isn't that 'Nannangadi'?"

"Yes, Nannangadi means the vessel of death."

Suddenly, he stopped, as if thinking about something.

This is what Brahmadevanandayogi said, "The only way out is through 'the vessel of death'"

"Come…" Rishi called Pappan and went to Kalichan Kavu. He said as he ran, "When I spoke to Brahmadevanandayogi, he said that the way out of here is only through the vessel of death. Nannangadi is the vessel of death. In Kalichan Kavu, beyond the holy wormwood tree, holy stone, and cave, there is a large rock in the forest where the waterfall begins. No one has yet gone there. Nannangadi is located at the top of the rock. Earlier, if someone died in the royal palace, they would be buried in that vessel. Such practices have been abandoned at present, and no one has visited there. That big vessel will be the way out of this place, where we are stuck. Even if there is not much hope, let us try it. This is our path, 'The vessel of death.'"

****

Chapter 34

King Bhimapalan dispatched troops in every direction. He also went out on a horseback. Eighteen regions were visited by the army troops. They looked everywhere, but were unable to locate Rishi and Pappan. One of the troops noticed smoke rising from a cliff close to Kalichan Kavu as they were making their way back. There followed the trail. Following the notification, Bhimapalan departed from Kalichan Kavu with soldiers.

If Bhimapalan caught them, Rishi and Pappan were sure to die.

****

Chapter 35

The waterfall was from a height of approximately 300 ft. It was a grand waterfall. A deep trench was located at the bottom. There was a cliff near the top of the waterfall and a bamboo grove with flowers.

Rishi and Pappan crossed the forest and reached the rock. They found Nannangadi there, a twenty-foot-tall, well-carved rock vessel on the cliff. The top was covered with a large flat stone. Nannangadi was carved into the shape of a large jar. The sounds of the animals were heard in the forest.

"If this is the vessel of death spoken of by Brahmadevanandayogi, then this is our way out."

They climbed by stacking stones near Nannangadi and moved the stone lid. It was just dark inside. Rishi looked at Pappan and said, "It's dark inside."

"The journey from one world to another will be full of darkness. We reached this world through darkness."

"We have no other option to choose. I am certain that this is the true choice," Rishi said.

Pappan held Rishi's hand and entered the pot. The falcon was flying overhead. When Rishi did not hear any sound from inside the pot, he loudly called Pappan. Only warm air was blowing outside.

Suddenly, with the sound of thunder, an arrow hit Rishi's shoulder. His feet slipped, and he fell to the ground. The stone lid moved itself and closed Nannangadi's mouth.

Raising his head, Rishi placed his fist on the floor. Half a dozen soldiers climbed the rocks and raced. He sprung to his feet and dashed toward them, jumping into the air, and he used the thumb of his foot to strike the forehead of one of the troops.

When a man brandished his sword, Rishi bent down and sat on his left knee. He caught the soldier by wrapping around his waist, and lifted him in the air to thwack him on rock. Suddenly, he grabbed a sword that had slipped from the soldier's hand and spun it several times in the air. Some archers were also wounded. Rishi looked around and saw that there were four soldiers left. One held a sword and the other held a bow. Rishi became more attentive by holding his sword in his hand parallel to the eye and moving his left leg backward and folding his right leg.

When an arrow pierced in the air, he struck it with the sword. The shield of one of the soldiers fell when Rishi spun in the air and hit him with the sword. He pulled the shield from the ground and threw it against another man; he fell to the valley. The soldiers could not keep pace with the lightning speed of the sword in Rishi's hands. One of the soldiers fell to the ground after being shot across the chest while raising his sword to strike Rishi. The other two soldiers fell to the ground within a few seconds and were unable to stand up to Rishi's martial splendour.

He turned around when he heard the sound of a horse. A man on a horse came over the hill; Bhimapalan stopped his horse and jumped down. He took the sword from the sheath and walked towards Rishi.

Although his vision was blurred due to bleeding on his face from the wound on his forehead, Rishi kicked with his left leg and picked up another sword. Rishi was ready with swords in both hands to fight Bhimapalan.

The darkness of the rain clouds, blowing sound of the storm, and roar of the waterfall created a tremendous atmosphere.

Lightning appeared in the sky.

Against Bhimapalan, Rishi rose into the air by pressing his right foot on the ground and, with one turn, slashed the sword with full vigor.

He had an injury in the left shoulder. He kicked Rishi with his right leg. Rishi fell down. He stood up even though he had hit his head on a large rock. The obscurity of sight made it difficult to identify the position of Bhimapalan, who came up with the sword again. Rishi ran on the rock on the left side and jumped in the air. He struck Bhimapalan with his sword, but Bhimapalan stopped him with his shield. However, Rishi rapidly slashed with a sword on his left hand. Blood trickled down from the side of Bhimapalan's neck. He punched Rishi with his dynamic left-hand. He slashed a sword at Rishi, who was lying on the ground. Rishi rolled on the ground and moved away.

Rishi realized that it was impossible to fight with the great, powerful, and martially skillful person. He fought with maximum ability.

He stood against Bhimapalan with swords on both hands.

Rishi stretched out his left hand and threw a sword towards him. While the sword was being knocked off, he inserted another sword into Bhimapalan's waist: Bhimapalan held him on the neck with strong hands. Rishi felt as if he had stopped breathing. He threw away Rishi and pulled out the sword from his waist.

Bhimapalan took a deep breath and took over another blood-stained sword from the ground to run towards Rishi with two swords. Rishi also picked up a sword lying on the ground. He was unable to resist it for a long time. His body had injury marks in several places. As Bhimapalan came forward, slashing the swords, Rishi had to move back.

With the sword in his hand, Rishi moved backwards and reached the edge of the rock. A wry smile spread across Bhimapalan's face. He shook his body, held swords in both hands, and approached Rishi. Before he could think of what to do next, Bhimapalan slashed him with the sword in his left hand. Rishi jumped backward from the edge of the cliff, or else the sword would have slid down his neck.

At the bottom of the waterfall was a deep trench. While felling, Rishi caught one bamboo stalk. The bamboo was bent down with his weight. He looked down while holding his left hand on a bamboo stalk. The water fell into the deep, trench. Bhimapalan came to the edge and looked at Rishi for a while, then he walked back. A little fear was starting to creep in. The distance from the crooked bamboo stalk to the rock was very much, but if he loosened his hand, he would have fallen into the abyss.

The muscles in his hands began to lose. He was unable to switch his hand to hold the bamboo stalk because he was holding a sword in his right hand. Rishi chopped the remaining bamboo with the sword and inserted it into the cut portion when the hand agony became intolerable. He was considering making his getaway when Bhimapalan, an enormous figure, reappeared on the cliff, holding the bow. He pointed to an arrow at Rishi's neck and stretched the bowstring as far as possible.

"Is this going to be my last?"

Slowly he closed his eyes. As soon as he heard the bowstring release sound, Rishi released his hand from the bamboo stalk. He fell into the abyss. When the weight of Rishi was released, the bamboo stick, which was bent, moved in the opposite direction. The sword of Rishi, which was inserted at the end of the bamboo, also splashed from the bamboo. The sword was fastened swiftly to the neck of Bhimapalan. His body fell into mud. There was a big lightning strike, and the thunder shook the air. A large bear exited the forestand came to Bhimapalan. It took Bhimapalan's body into its hands and walked slowly back into the forest.

There was peace on Rishi's face as he went down with the waterfall. Even as he plunged into the abyss, several moments flashed across his memory.

The stone steps by the pool were climbed by two feet and a black mole on the ankle of one foot.

A lovely girl circled a sacred wormwood tree.

The lamp at ' Kalmandapu' was lit by a kind hand-wearing bangles.

The beautiful face was brightened by light from the lamp.

A beautiful girl was coming with a garland.

However, Rishi was unable to recognize any of these faces.

Deeper in the water, he drowned.

****

Chapter 36

The next morning, the armed Serchas stormed into the palace. They released Vijayapalan from the prison. Serchas had a mob behind them.

Later, the *Bharana Niyamavali* was placed on a stand at the centre of the palace hall.

Scholars began to explain to the people of villages about the Bharana Niyamavali.

In each of the villages, people began to choose them to rule over them.

Chanthan was elected as leader at his village. The new era of Thali began there.

****

Chapter 37

Rishi was sinking further into the abyss. The last air bubbles inside him escaped through his nose and mouth, rising toward the surface. Darkness covered his memories.

****

Chapter 38

The ECG readout showed that the ECG had become abnormal. The duty physician and two nurses hurried to the intensive care unit when the nurse, worried, sounded an alarm. When Deepa heard the disturbance, she woke up from her nap in a chair in the hallway. Deepa peered inside through the glass in the centre of the intensive care unit door. Rishi was being examined by the doctor with a stethoscope. Rishi's pulse was being monitored by a nurse. Electrocardiogram was flat.

Deepa picked up her mobile phone and called it Raghavan. There was a feeling that something was about to go wrong. Rishi had been in the ICU for more than a week. Dr. Alexander called every day from the United States.

The doctor applied an electro conductive gel to the device, called the defibrillator, and held it parallel to Rishi's chest. By the time he counted down, "Three, two, one," the nurse had pressed the switch on the electrical current to the defibrillator, applied the device to Rishi's chest, and retracted it a second later. The same procedure was repeated three or four times; however, there was no response from the body. The electrocardiogram was completely straight. The doctor walked out of the ICU. The nurse closed Rishi's eyes with her right palm.

She had no mental strength to hear the doctor. She leaned on the door and sobbed. There was silence all around. While trying to get rid of the leash attached to Rishi's head, the nurse noticed a slight change in the screen of the electroencephalogram. The thin lines on the screen are dancing by making hills and craters.

"His Brain Function started working,"The nurse said. The doctors and nurses looked with anticipation and excitement.

Suddenly Rishi jerked up on the bed and sucked in as much air as he could.

The ECG graph also begun to produce waves. He gasped. There was a look of surprise on the doctor's face while entering the room. The nurse who checked Rishi's pulse said, "The pulse starts becoming normal."

Deepa entered into the room after the doctor. Rishi opened his eyes and tried to look over.

"Where am I? What happened to me?"

A nurse held Deepa, who was crying on his chest.

Rishi effort fully identified every person around him. Suddenly, Rishi asked about Pappan.

"Where's Pappan?"

"Pappan is in the next room. He regained consciousness. Health is improving."Deepa said.

The doctor opened his eyelids and examined his iris.

"How're you?"

"Better."

"Can you remember? What's been happening these days?"

Rishi slowly closed his eyes.

"Doctor, it looks like darkness. Nothing is clear. Sometimes I can hear something like the sound of anklets."

The doctor and Deepa looked at each other.

Rishi opened his eyes and smiled at them.

****

Chapter 39

His head rested on his palm as he lay on the floor beneath a tree in Kavu. The area was bathed in the reddish glow of the evening sun. Thechirping of birds filled the air.

"I can't get back the memories I had when I was in a coma. Doctors said that such memories rarely come back. However, the anklet sound was haunting. Still, I can experience it again."

He opened his eyes and got up from the floor.

"The same chime, the voice of anklet."

When he heard a whistle, Rishi searched for it.

One of the Narayan flowers rolled over and fell onto Rishi. He heard an anklet chime. Rishi walked over and stopped near the pavement where he hears the sound. He shifted the vines infront his face and looked at the pavement.

A beautiful young girl in a yellow blouse and dark green skirt held a basket full of wildflowers. She stepped onto the stone steps at the end of the pavement. With each pace, a chime sound was produced. Rishi descended to the pavement and watched her from behind. She climbed the stairs at each step. Rishi looked at her and noticed a black mole on her foot beneath the anklet. Then a cold breeze blew, and Narayan flowers fell between them.

****

www.ingramcontent.com/pod-product-compliance
Lightning Source LLC
LaVergne TN
LVHW041842070526
838199LV00045BA/1402